An Eye for an Eye and Your Other Eye and the Rest of Your Family

A Duke Dasher Novel

D1714336

MARK BALDACCI

ISBN: 9781695131125

This book is absurdist satire. Nothing in the
following text is remotely accurate or true. It is
merely reheated bathwater bleeding onto the
page from a lunatic's pen. Sickly manifestations
birthed from bouts of night terrors and Sutter
Home minis. Names, characters, businesses,
places, events, locales, and incidents either are
the products of the author's unwell imagination
or used in a fictitious manner. Any resemblance
to actual persons, living or dead, or actual
events is purely coincidental. Create nothing.
Consume Everything.

CONTENTS

ACKNOWLEDGMENTS

This book is dedicated to anyone who has ever read a single word on One Tie All Tie. To Laura who convinced me to write in the first place, to all of my friends for eternally supporting me and to Blood and Mumsie who always believed that someday I would fulfill my dream of being a surfing artist.

For more stories visit http://www.onetie-alltie.com

Book design by SueJanna Truscott
More incredible design work: https://www.suejanna.com

Edited with protest by Eva Paulson

1 A GOD FEARING MAN

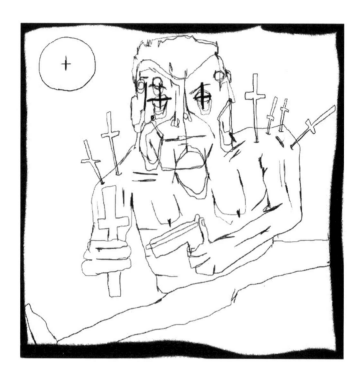

Rockford,
Illinois,
United States

Duke Dasher woke up at 3:30 a.m., as he did every morning, with a military issued Glock 19 (safety off) resting in each hand. The only way for a real patriot and ex-Special Ops member to wake up. Though his wife Stacy had expressed concerns about sleeping with loaded guns in each hand, Dasher assured her he would sleep just fine. "Who needs sleeping pills or a nice mattress when you've got guns?" Dasher told Stacy, flicking off the lamp with one of the Glocks. Stacy would lay awake for hours listening to the steel of the Glocks rubbing together, praying they would survive another night. He brewed his usual cup of black coffee, the only thing he drank before reading several verses from his leather-bound Bible. The county's last Democratic President had bestowed the Bible upon him after Dasher murdered an imposter of that very President trying to blow up the White House several years earlier. Dasher attempted to remember the name of the President, but it ultimately alluded him, as the candidate was non-Republican and thus inconsequential. He considered the ease with which the Democrat was impersonated - bleeding heart liberals would trust any bootlicking pushover who was willing to stroke their fragile egos.

He turned the Bible over in his hands and threw it up in the air before unloading both clips into the book. Stacy woke immediately, in a complete panic, wondering why a gun was emptied in their bedroom. She looked at her husband Duke who stood menacingly over the book. He walked calmly back to bed and laid down next to her still holding the pistols. He stroked a loose strand of hair behind her ear, a tried and true way to pacify someone after demolishing a booby-trapped Bible with a barrage of bullets. He calmly explained that the former President had likely planted a bomb in the book. It would be just like some spineless Democrat to wait for an opportune time to detonate it and kill the family. Even though it was a holy book, it had to be destroyed; someone who could never be trusted had compromised it. Stacy could not make sense of the sudden irrational paranoia nor the unorthodox method for defusing the alleged bomb. Instead of arguing, she simply nodded, staring deeply at the smoldering book remains on the ground. "He's not our President any more honey, nothing to worry about," Dasher said, as he unloaded one final bullet into the book.

He pulled a fresh copy from his bedside drawer and calmed himself down by reading a few verses. The words helped soothe him as he began reading about the vengeful God he knew and loved. He had personally cut out the New Testament from every one of his Bibles with a machete, knowing damn well that God had gone soft in that version, his message disappointingly flaccid in comparison to the awesome power of a murderous omnipotent being cleansing the earth of evildoers. New Testament God was the reason Christianity was failing in Dasher's mind. No one wants a God who is approachable and reasonable. They want unpredictable and ruthless. Dasher had responsibly wielded that same power for his country over the past decade, but had since retired to become a devoted stay-at-home father. A job more important than the most top-secret military force ever assembled. Though upon further reflection, he deemed it far less critical than carelessly mowing down hordes of terrorists with different assault weapons, sharp and blunt objects, and in some cases, his massive calloused hands. Dasher stood at 6 foot 8 inches and weighed a hefty 260 pounds, a crew cut and absolutely no tattoos, cut like the Statue of David (if he knew what that was).

Dasher despised all art, religious or not, because of its frivolousness and its tendency for deviation from family, and country. The best way to worship and celebrate God was not artistic expression. It was sitting in a balmy church room with a productive cough and being tongue lashed by a dying priest who considers you an unsalvageable heathen.

"Morning dad!" screamed Terry Dasher, his 5-year-old son.

"You know the rules, stand silently while I finish this final Bible verse," replied Dasher lovingly.

Terry stood for several more minutes in total awkward silence as Dasher finished his lengthy morning ritual. It was time for breakfast. Dasher asked Terry what he would like for breakfast before promptly serving him the same thing they ate every morning: three hard-boiled eggs and a glass of room temperature water. The two enjoyed breakfast together, talking about varying terrorist attacks around the globe, how to sharpen knives properly, and the prospect of taking another man's life with your bare hands.

The most recent attack was a mysterious slaying in Paris; over two dozen people lay dead with their necks snapped. No other evidence existed; the scene appeared haunting, to say the least.

"Why do these piece-of-shit cowards do it, Terry? You tell me. Is it foolish pride? Jealousy? Maybe they are just too dumb to do anything else. Something about this latest one just isn't sitting right," said Dasher, alone grinding his teeth. Five-year-old Terry stood there, uncertain how to answer the extremely complex and nuanced question asked by his father.

Dasher waited several seconds, staring at Terry, hoping for a response that would never come. He shook his head in disappointment and went back to watching television. Thousands of miles away Dasher's questions were being answered in an ISIS cloning facility.

Baghdad,
Iraq

Vladimir Popov sat in an abandoned ISIS cloning facility. A Russian businessman with a murky past and a propensity to get blackout drunk and lose his shit. A full-blown alcoholic who loved only two things in life: communism and the drink. The facility had been shut down and abandoned after the terrorist organization was only successful in cloning a mini horse-human hybrid. It was an unsettling looking creature, to say the least, with a somber human-looking face, sunken eyes, and continuously pursed lips. Its hooves were covered in varying sizes of toenails. The animal was too friendly for war and very temperamental, so they had cut their losses and focused on other things. Popov saw potential in the facility though; an opportunity for the Russians to genetically engineer a new type of super-soldier if all went according to plan. The problem with the terrorist organization previously running it was their obsession with creating what they deemed to be a warhorse, a horse with human intelligence. When in actuality, the facility could have just as easily manufactured genetically superior humans with the mere flick of a switch. Popov had found only one person left in the facility, an obsessed mad man who refused to let the project die and known only by the name Hisan.

Popov had taken the young man under his wing, promising to give him powers beyond his wildest imagination. Abilities that would let him seek revenge against the country that refused to let him run his horse-forward experiments. The United States would pay for preventing the world from experiencing his glorious creatures and his way of life.

Since finding the weak scientist several years ago, and immediately beginning enhancement experimentation, Hisan had become even more powerful than Popov could have ever foreseen. His willingness to push his physical and emotional boundaries was fascinating.

The keystone of his desire for torture, pain and hasty genetic enhancements were derived from a singular source.

Driven by pure hatred towards a single country - the United States of America.

Hisan longed for the mini horses he had raised from birth; he sought a world where humans and mini horse hybrids coexisted peacefully, building cities together in harmony. Sometimes even crossbreeding if the scenario presented itself.

With the rabid experimentations run by Popov, Hisan had grown to 7 foot 3 inches tall, his bones strong as titanium, his muscle fibers repaired five times faster than normal humans, and his reflexes were anything but human. His entire body marred in varying scars and brandings from the extensive surgeries and experiments and his head cleanly shaved, Hisan was exactly what Popov needed to create chaos. And he had done just that. Following orders from Popov, Hisan had begun several attacks around the world, including the most recently executed attack in Paris, which had found its way to Dasher's television set. Testing and honing his abilities, the attack in Paris left two dozen people dead and several hundred commemorative Eiffel Tower themed berets urinated on and burned. Popov was impressed with his progress, but was he ready to topple the most powerful government in the world? Likely not. The infrastructure of the country was flimsy enough, but it needed to be further weakened.

Popov flicked a cigarette effortlessly to the ground and walked to the containment tank that held Hisan. The tank itself had been bought second hand from Criss Angel and was said to have unique healing properties. The magician had fallen on hard times and was forced to sell the decorative tank before it got repossessed. Even a magician as talented as Criss Angel couldn't escape a lifetime of irresponsible spending habits. He had even thrown in a few mesh Ed Hardy shirts and several sets of heavily used leather pants to sweeten the deal as Popov gladly took the enchanted chamber off his hands. If the chamber gave one Las Vegas-based magician the power of levitation, imagine what it could do for a super-soldier going through a constant stream of enrichment surgeries and experiments. He took an enormous bubbling pull from a plastic handle of well vodka and swallowed it with ease.

He tapped on the tank like a child on the fish tank at a dentist's office.

"Soon enough my friend, soon enough," said Popov as Hisan's eyes blinked open, full of rage.

Rockford,
Illinois,
United States

Dasher gazed out of the window at his perfectly landscaped lawn, noticing his neighbor's yard hadn't been mowed in several days. Dasher considered the neighbor a failure as a man and more importantly, as a citizen of this country. Dasher likened the bent grass blades to football players kneeling during the national anthem, and there was nothing more disrespectful to the flag than a neglected lawn. He contemplated a physical confrontation but ultimately decided to do 1000 burpees with a knife in his mouth instead. Dasher took every opportunity to train, especially now that he was a stay-at-home dad and could feel his edge growing ever softer. But not too soft. His name preceded him in Rockford and there was always a tough guy looking to prove himself. Dasher would sometimes sit around at bars in the city; even though he did not drink, he did enjoy a good fountain diet Sprite and contributing to the local economy. On several occasions, patrons who had picked fights ended up in a choke out with a pomegranate Michelob Ultra up their ass before being morally eviscerated with a fire and brimstone lecture. Though the person lay unconscious and unable to retain any of Dasher's misinformed Bible teachings, Dasher would preach on, sometimes even asking questions and growing more enraged when a response didn't come. If the person didn't answer quickly enough, Dasher would more often than not resort to routine water-boarding, which was equally ineffective in terms of getting repentance from an unconscious bar patron.

His wife worked as a pro bono doctor at a hospital for orphaned children. Sweeter than apple pie and said to have inspired the entire Open Hearts jewelry collection at Kay Jewelers. Dasher had sworn to her never to take a mission again, but how long could he actually last as an ordinary civilian? Especially with these strange murders taking place across the globe. How long before those reached his hallowed soil? Stacy found Dasher's bloodlust endearing, and it was part of the reason she married him, but the birth of their son had made her more protective of Duke than ever.

Dasher was honorably discharged from Special Ops after he refused direct orders to leave his partner behind after they had been ambushed and outnumbered 100 to one. Instead, Dasher had infiltrated the group and silently beheaded the leader of the terrorist organization. Using his face as a mask, he commanded the rest of the troop to commit suicide, and like the cowards Dasher assumed they were, they dutifully obeyed.

When he had ripped off the skin mask, even his partner, Luke Riley, puked several times. Dasher held out his hand for a high five with a heartwarming blood-soaked grin. His enormous white teeth were in stark contrast to the blackened blood that filled every pore on the rest of his face. He had gone back to the barracks that night and reenacted the moment using warmed slices of pimento loaf and Greek yogurt to mimic the mutilated face. Troop members who had been shaken up by the whole ordeal laughed sheepishly and sipped whiskey, hoping that Dasher would grow tired of the insane charade. Dasher took their polite laughter as whole-hearted encouragement and continued to dance around; mocking the incident for several more hours before finally suggesting the group join him in an equally awkward group prayer.

Looking back on the incident...the scene was as grotesque as they came and though his partner was successfully extracted, news outlets covering the incident had found it to be one of the most disturbing ever seen. Dasher had watched the footage of the incident played by CNN years later and couldn't understand the backlash. It was a mission completed with surgical precision and what media outlet wouldn't love a good ole fashioned mass terrorist suicide by way of elaborate disguise? It was a feel good story by every classification of the genre. *Classic leftist news outlets* thought Dasher, always putting their backward narrative on even the most wholesome acts of heroism. How could the media spin something so beautiful, something so intuitive, something so American? Dasher's hatred and mistrust for the news grew in the years following, to the point where he started a news station of his own on an AM radio; but, most of the reporting eventually devolved into rants about the dangers of contraceptives in regards to women's suffrage and the myriad of biblical inaccuracies portrayed in Russell Crowe's 2014 adaptation of Noah.

Dasher's commanding officer, Tom Watley, had commended Dasher for his ingenuity, but because he disobeyed a director order, he was ultimately cast out of his Special Forces unit. Looking back on the incident, Dasher wouldn't have changed a damn thing. It was the world that was changing, not him, and when a threat became too severe for this new softer world, Dasher would be waiting in the wings ready to saw the face off whatever the problem was.

"Come on, son, time to get some groceries," Dasher said to Terry as they hopped into their 2005 Chevy Silverado.

If it ain't broke, don't fix it, thought Dasher as they drove to the store together. Dasher and his son headed through the town they had come to know and love. The lifeless suburb pacified Dasher to a point. It had painstakingly smoothed out most of his rough edges and distinguishing

16

features, grinding him into a purposeless beige orb used to decorate a rarely used home office. The only things he was capable of focusing on was his lawn, his God, and his family. All and all a passable life indeed for most, but something was still missing. Maybe it was the murdering, but he couldn't determine that at the moment. At the checkout line, Dasher caught a glimpse of a small tube television behind the counter. As the clerk checked over several tons of knuckle steak and a single onion, Dasher noticed something disturbing.

"Turn that up, NOW," Dasher yelled to the clerk.

The news reporter stated what Dasher already knew. The most recent incident was the first of its kind on American soil. Thirty people at the Mall of America, all dead, all with their necks snapped. Not a single drop of evidence at the crime scene. No one knew why or how these killings were happening, but someone had to find out soon.

Dasher hawked an enormous wad of spit on the ground at the grocery store, drawing the eyes of several concerned customers. The customers looked down at the watery gobbet and back up at Dasher before returning to the pulsating wad. The bubbles of the loogie gazed back at them with similar distrust, eventually popping into the dank air of the supermarket.

"Watch him," repeated Dasher to the clerk.
"Beg your pardon, sir?" said the clerk.
"Watch him," repeated Dasher, more sternly pointing at his son Terry.

"Sir, I'm only 16 years old, and I have no idea who you are…" squeaked the clerk.

"I'll be back as soon as I can, for once in your life, be somebody kid," interrupted Dasher as he was already in a full wind sprint back to his Silverado. Time to get Watley on the horn. Could it really be…him?

2 THE RISE OF HISAN

Somewhere outside of the Mall of America, Minnesota, United States

"Another successful mission, my child," said Popov to a kneeling, fully nude Hisan.

The sick bastard had just carried out one of the most deadly attacks on American soil in recent history. If the entire earth's population were welded together into one unintelligible mass that was vaguely Christian and had a healthy hatred of any ideological differences, atrocities like this would never happen. Fortunately, for Popov, fantasies like this only existed in the righteous mind of Duke Dasher, who was currently white knuckling his way across the country. Likely listening to the *Left Behind* series on cassette, narrated by Kirk Cameron, to torque himself up for a confrontation with whoever was committing these atrocities.

"Twelve more attacks should suffice," continued Popov, feeding Hisan a bottle of Vodka like a caring mother feeding a baby.

Hisan's lips greedily latched onto the bottle of vodka, sucking deeply on its cracking nipple. On top of being a terrorist, Hisan was, of course, also a full-blown alcoholic. Popov had raised him as most Russians were built, on grain alcohol, raw potatoes, and a healthy longing for a return to communist glory. The only thing more dangerous than an alcoholic terrorist was a sober terrorist, so in this case, Hisan was slightly less dangerous than a sober

20

terrorist was. Still undoubtedly very dangerous and with the enhancements made by Popov, certainly a formidable enemy for Dasher. Popov had called Hisan back to the basement of a Chili's Too an hour south of the Mall of America. They had to meet to discuss the final phases of their precious plan.

This shrouded meeting lasted for several hours. Varying blueprints were observed and a routine flogging of Hisan was done to remind him of his loyalty. Several other members of Popov's communist recruits looked on disapprovingly, as the relationship had grown in perversion. They realized that Popov was someone who would never back down; he was willing to go through any lengths to achieve his goal of toppling the most powerful and honorable government ever constructed. The Obama years were but a minor blemish on an otherwise unscathed country history. The meeting concluded with several cities circled in red on a map. Popov opened a curtain behind them to reveal a room filled with a thousand soldiers standing in line and at attention. A banquet hall for the communist revolution, complete with obligatory Bloomin Onions and molten lava cakes.

"These men shall ride you to freedom…to the start new world Hisan…my horse," said Popov with a tear in his eye.

Nearby guards looked at each other, puzzled by the phrasing. The next point of attack formed the backbone of American ideals and was referred to by many as the birthplace of democracy, Noah's Ark waterpark in Wisconsin Dells.

Bloomington, Minnesota, United States

Dasher rolled down the window on the 2010 H3 Hummer he borrowed from the supermarket parking lot. He needed something with a little more power than his Silverado. Saving the environment could wait. He certainly didn't trust the concept of anything electric or foreign, so he drove onward in the hulking yellow Hummer. White knuckling the steering wheel, he had to make it to Minnesota. Dasher wondered what kind of a sick, ignorant fuck would carry out an attack on something as innocent as a shopping mall?

Moreover, the largest mall in the world at that, with a goddamn roller coaster inside of it. What did Yankee Candle have to do with international turmoil? Why was Build-A-Bear workshop the catalyst for some of the greatest atrocities committed on American soil?

Dasher lit a cigarette and put it out, a ritual he had picked up during his time with his Special Forces unit. A testament to the ultimate control he had over his body and mind - an authority that few men had, even inside his elite unit, and even fewer outside the borders of America. As Dasher approached the Minnesota skyline, something from his past vaguely haunted him.

An almost indeterminable feeling. Buried under blind consumption of fire and brimstone and relentless posturing, something stirred.

Seeking out feelings was something that did not interest Dasher. He considered the concept of therapy as much of a conspiracy as vaccinating your children. Anyone trying to get inside of your mind, even in an effort to heal, was not to be trusted. The bloated walrus taking notes on your innermost feelings was almost certainly a spy, paid to collect information on you for the Russians. Something created for snowflake Millennials whom he despised as much, if not more than the terrorists. Little bastards who spent their entire lives behind the comfort of a keyboard, fighting wars of no consequence. Why didn't they believe in the same things he did? Making the country better, obsessively worshipping the Lord and Savior Jesus Christ, and eradicating terrorist threats. Considering the simplicity of it only increased the rage growing within Dasher. These sniveling little insects were too obsessed with avocado toast and Instagram "likes" to worry about surgically removing threats to their country and strong-arming others into Christianity. If the New Testament didn't exist for Dasher, neither would Millennials, and this world would be a hell of a lot better off.

When Dasher was forced into military-mandated therapy after hundreds of incidents, which would suggest a full loss of sanity, he sat as stoic as ever. He would place his pistol on the mahogany table between him and the therapist and sit with his arms crossed in silence until the required time was up. After the awkward exchange had mercifully concluded, he would fire a round into the ceiling and walk out with a smirk on his face. This therapist would never crack him. As much as he begged and pleaded, Dasher wouldn't concede an inch; he had been through far more hellacious interrogations than this. If the therapist wanted some information, he would have to ram bamboo shoots under his fingernails and toenails, and even then, it was unlikely he would give anything up. He would drive home happily to a wife and kid who had, unbeknownst to him, grown oppositely quite unhappy.

Dasher pulled into the mall parking lot, the caution tape still flapping in the wind. A sudden cold had settled in as the gnarled fingers of old man winter desperately fondled the throat of the Midwest. Dasher jumped out of his car and blew into his hands, trying to generate some warmth. Steam flew from his Styrofoam coffee cup. He saluted the police officers on the scene. Show respect for anyone wearing a uniform, thought Dasher as he somberly nodded at another officer at the scene. Dasher was well known by damn near everyone in any military, police, or government entity, as he routinely attended charity functions and saved asses whenever given the opportunity.

He approached the scene and took a closer look at the bodies; there was no way any human could have done this. Maybe at one time they were human, but not now. A monster did this. Even with his enormous hands, unreal stamina and lust for blood, Dasher could not have achieved this type of destruction and death. A fit of primal and misplaced jealousy ignited within Dasher. He had to admit, the scene was impressive.

He put a cigarette in his mouth and took it out, furiously throwing it to the ground. He put his blue tooth in his ear and rang his old pal Tom Watley.

"Watley, Dasher here...this is going to be fun," he said, holding and kissing his signature silver cross necklace.

Wisconsin Dells,
United States,
Noah's Ark Waterpark

Hisan sat with his newly minted army in the damp basement of Noah's Ark Waterpark. A group of men ready to give it all for communism and the fear of being horribly beaten if Popov got drunk enough. The basement reeked like the piss filling the pools above. Hisan hated what waterparks stood for: empty consumerism and massive plastic funneling devices, both pinnacles of western ideology. The mission from Popov had been to destroy the waterpark by any means necessary. To humiliate the lard asses mainlining cotton candy funnel cakes and absorbing foot-long corn dogs as suppositories. Destroying the country's waterslide infrastructure was like taking away its veins and arteries, and thus, its heart.

Popov, whose goal was to ransack everything the country loved, had methodically selected the set of targets. If people did not feel safe bringing their kids to a loosely monitored waterpark with questionable safety regulations and semi-regular drownings, they would not feel safe anywhere. They had infiltrated the waterpark by buying tickets and entering the park as any reasonable person

25

would. The security measures were limited to one person managing towel distribution as if it were the last day of their life. The entire army of fully-grown men had gone more or less unnoticed, as no one dared exceed the allotment of one towel per person. The only rule at a waterpark worth abiding by. The group of men had raised suspicion amongst several other pool attendees. The vestige of joy in their eyes, which was still minimal, seemed out of place in the confines of somewhere usually void of happiness. The suspicions were ultimately cast aside however, as each observer ultimately came to the conclusion that the group was simply already drunk enough to endure the waterpark as it was. Despite some protests from other members of the revolution, who would have preferred not to sit in the swampy taint of a waterpark, Hisan considered the underlying basement and tunnel system the perfect place to reflect on the mission. Before the end of the day, every one of those floundering carnival goldfish-in-a-bags would have his or her neck snapped. They were all indirectly responsible for what had happened all those years ago to Hisan's beloved creatures. They would each experience what those horse-hybrids experienced that night. Pure and utter terror and more pain than humanly imaginable.

As parents dug themselves further and further into debt and kids chose the pool in favor of a trip to the bathroom, Hisan and his army of shadows waited for the perfect opportunity.

There was a crackle in Hisan's earpiece.

"Hisan, what the hell are you doing? It is neck-snapping time!" Popov shouted through the Circuit City earpiece that had been permanently implanted in Hisan's head after some objection.

Hisan took one final pull from the handle of vodka he had been drinking, stood up, and rallied the troops. Popov hadn't been wrong yet, and Hisan trusted him in everything he did. Hisan's scientist brain was still adapting to revenge and carnage, and Popov was the perfect manipulator.

Bloomington, Minnesota, United States

Dasher was awakened in the middle of the night by the sound of his cell phone ringing. "Wanted Dead or Alive," a song that he had spent several frustrating weekends trying to program as his ringtone, played loudly. He came to covet that sound, even in the middle of the night, when he knew it meant he was going to have to raise hell. Maybe it was those times he cherished more than anything. During the day, his phone ringing meant another soul-crushing errand dictated by Stacy or even worse, a conversation with his son. The night, however, was unpredictable and erratic. The ringing could mean virtually anything. There was nothing better than waking up to the gentle sound that is accompanied by the anticipation of violence in the name of God. On those nights, the moon seemed to glow even brighter.

"It's Dasher, talk to me," he barked into his Motorola Razr.

Dasher did not trust smartphones. He saw them as a sign of weakness and distraction. In Dasher's mind, technology, in general, was something that removed us further from our ancestors. Distracting us from feeling, reprogramming our minds into a gonzo money shot aggregator. All of our thoughts and feelings suffocated and drowned in favor of the endless scroll. Oftentimes rolling the content spewing from our phone between our fattened fingers like a ball of snot before timidly sneaking it into our already brimming cheeks. A surprisingly emotionally intelligent observation from Dasher.

Dasher's wife had once brought home a pair of smartphones as a surprise anniversary gift. The phone was loaded with all of Dasher's favorite music. She even had speed dials programmed for their pastor and his parents. Upon seeing them, Dasher instantly threw the phones in the microwave and set the timer for 30 minutes. He stood and maniacally watched the spinning glass plate until the thirty minutes were up. He had to make sure both the phones and microwave were utterly destroyed. Stacy had sadly gone back to watching reruns of JAG, her act of kindness completely squandered.

"Dasher, it's Watley. You better get ready for this," said Watley.

Watley went on to describe the complete and utter carnage that had occurred at Noah's Ark waterpark in the

Wisconsin Dells. Dasher listened in horror as Watley kept making a bizarre clicking noise with his tongue when describing the neck snappings at the water park. Dasher's fury grew with each nauseating click.

"Watley, what the hell is that clicking noise?" growled Dasher into the phone.

"Everyone's necks were snapped Dasher, not a single bullet. Just someone snapping the necks of several hundred people and then rearranging the corpses into the Russian flag," continued Watley, pushing through the awkward silence of Dasher's heavy breathing.

He clicked his tongue several more times in a row. They were always one step behind. But how? The United States and by extension, Dasher, was never one step behind. Ever one step ahead - always pushing the boundaries of freedom and justice.

"Shut the fuck up, Watley, and let me think! Also, would you cool it with that clicking noise! I know damn well what a neck-snapping sounds like, and that little click you're doing is doing it no justice at all. The sound of you slobbering all over yourself is making me sicker than the mass murder that just happened," said Dasher, momentarily losing his composure.

"Sorry Watley. I know several hundred people being brutally murdered isn't necessarily your fault, but anytime the United States gets one pulled over on it like this, we are all responsible. If we all believed in the one true God, had a healthy fear of all immigrants, an aggressively Republican President, and wiped the Obama years from all history books, this shit wouldn't happen," continued Dasher over the sound of his teeth grinding.

"Look, I completely agree Dasher. I think 99% of the world agrees with that, but it won't change what happened. The only evidence we have is drone footage of what appears to be someone or something leading the attack; it's …huge," said Watley as he stared at the footage. "I'm forwarding it to the Roku in your hotel room now."

Dasher wrestled with the remote for the better part of the afternoon. Outside of dutifully watching Joel Oscreen's morning service from time to time, Dasher never turned on the television. The concept of remaining completely idle while being spoon-fed content displeased Dasher. Not to mention the clearly leftist bias which plagued virtually every program available, save Sunday Service with Joel Oscreen. Joel Oscreen was a celebrity pastor that had risen in fame for looking and sounding like another celebrity pastor. He looked like a very poorly made version of the other pastor, with even larger veneers that hung from his bleeding gums like loose dominos and uncommonly tanned skin that seemed to continually need adjusting to stay in place. Most of his program, *So, You're Going to Hell, Now what?*, was spent frantically kneading and maneuvering his chapped skin, which seemed willing to melt from his slight frame at a moment's notice. When he did speak, his voice sounded like the hissing of a nitrous tank, instilling fear and humiliation into whoever was willing to indulge in a huff. The public disregarded the peculiarity and accepted him without question. They were too focused on making donations to Oscreen's church, which was said to be the easiest way to avoid damnation. Dasher liked a good bargain in life and a knockoff human suited him just fine. He found the constant skin adjustments to be a charming ode to the lepers he read about in the Bible. Oscreen also focused more on fire and brimstone, personal shame and condemnation than the other pastor did, so Dasher was a predictably staunch supporter.

If Dasher had it his way, *Kids Say the Darndest Things* would rot in hell with the entire CNN catalog of programming. Why would anyone watch TV when someone had written something as incredible as the Bible? Or recite the Pledge of Allegiance? Or be a faithful husband and a caring father? Finally, after several hours of praying and a little luck, Dasher managed to get the footage up on the television.

"It's him," muttered Dasher aloud, shattering the remote in his enormous hands.

Recalling a memory he thought he had vanquished from his mind long ago, he rubbed his temples and searched frantically through swarms of old homilies, paranoia involving the Obama family being lizard people and countless missions where he saved his entire team's asses. Then it hit him.

Several years ago, he had taken an elite group of mercenaries deep into the heart of Baghdad, intending to destroy a facility that was allegedly capable of producing human-animal hybrids. What he saw was a bunch of sick cucks trying to play God and doing a piss-poor job at it, for there is only one true all-powerful, all-knowing Man, who created everything around us. Four mini horses with the faces of human beings sat lazily around a slop pen, feasting on what appeared to be human entrails. Dasher vomited instantly and moved stealthily closer. He noticed a lone scientist extracting blood and stool samples from the despicable looking beings. The scientist looked up and locked eyes with Dasher. Dasher sprinted at him, despite the fact that he was unarmed and had his hands in the air. The rest of the team stood and watched as Dasher picked up a full head of steam. He approached the scientist, drew his gun and hurled it as hard as he could at the scientist's face. The glock was immediately absorbed by the soft face of the horse lover, shattering his nose into a thousand bone pieces, which fell to the floor, along with his teeth, like shards of glass.

"Hell of a catch scientist, you ever consider playing for the Yankees?" Dasher asked the man writhing around in a growing pool of his own blood.

He turned back and grinned at his troop, who were now translucently pale and looked on the verge of tears. Must not like baseball, thought Dasher. Their loss.

The scientist tried to explain to Dasher that the facility had been converted into a sanctuary for these creatures, but after several rounds of relentless waterboarding on his already mangled face and a few carefully curated lessons from the Bible, Dasher got him to admit otherwise.

32

"Tell me about these piece of shit horses, scumbag!"
Dasher yelled as the horse abominations looked at the
interrogation uninterestedly.

The scientist refused to crack until finally, Dasher was left
with no choice. He grabbed one of the mini horses and
firmly planted his standard issue Glock at the back of its
mane. The horse looked up with no discernable emotion,
merely grazing on the last of the slop in front of it. Dasher
clicked the trigger on the gun, hoping to instill fear in the
horse who still had no reaction.

"You tell me how these things are going to wreak havoc
on the United States or this thing's brains are going to
become dinner for his friends. I don't want to have to do
this, but so help me God, I will," Dasher said, regaining
his composure.

The scientist had to think on his feet to convince this
lunatic that these horses had experienced enough suffering
in their lifetime. They hadn't asked to be created the way
they were - a living abomination to most.

"Ok! These were trained as reconnaissance horses that
would eventually be trained to murder the President's child
at the annual White House county fair!" The scientist
screamed, hoping the false admittance would be a plausible
answer for the lunatic in front of him.

Dasher snickered and then stared pensively at the horses.
Though they were horrific, they were still technically God's
creatures, as anything living on this earth is,

33

excluding enemies of the United States and anyone he held a personal vendetta against. He was overcome with an immense feeling of sorrow for the creatures and decided they would live their best life if they were free - roaming the desert and prancing about at will. The scientist pleaded with Dasher as he opened the warehouse doors, saying that the horses were in no way prepared to live outside of the facility. They were gentle creatures with no understanding of hardship, completely uncorrupted by the world outside. Everyone else in the room seemed to understand that a single minute in the cruel desert would kill them immediately, but Dasher patted each one on the ass, an indication that it was time for them to jog to freedom.

One collapsed instantly into a sandpit, breaking all of its legs and unleashing a horrible, continuous cry, while wolves immediately slaughtered the others, as the scientist looked on completely dismayed. The wolves ripping and tearing at the faces of the hybrids who desperately wept for their master would haunt the desert wind for years to come.

"They would rather die standing than live on their knees," Dasher said in a patriotic tone, irrelevant to the current situation.

When he turned around, ready to send the scientist straight to hell to live in pain and suffering with his creatures, the scientist had vanished. Distracted by the slaughter and the sound of a horrifying human hybrid horse screaming, Dasher had allowed the scientist to escape.

Now that same man was wreaking havoc on America. Although he had changed in every way, physically enormous and bloodthirsty, Dasher still recognized his face immediately. It was the face of a man who had loved his human-horse hybrids, maybe a little too much. It was a man consumed by hatred. Though Dasher recalled the prior confrontation, he in no way considered there to be a correlation between what had happened all those years ago and what was happening now. This sick bastard would have always done this; nothing Dasher did or did not do would have changed that. Each man was in charge of his own destiny, with help from God and the Holy Spirit of course. Now Dasher would have to do what he could not do all those years ago and finally kill the scientist.

3 The Worst Cracker Barrel in the Country

Wisconsin Dells, Wisconsin, United States

"Very good Hisan," Popov said in the parking lot of a Cracker Barrel located just outside of the water park where they had just slaughtered dozens of innocent people.

"Yes, master, though we suffered several casualties," replied Hisan, slightly worried.

"As it turns out, most of the people there had concealed carry-arms tucked into their ill-fitting board shorts and were looking for a reason to use them. We lost eight men to one single man wearing a Life is Good shirt," continued Hisan, shocked at the readiness for someone to both bring an armed gun to a waterpark and be willing to unload it at the first sign of unknown danger.

Popov had anticipated this; he was always one step ahead. He knew this was not going to be an easy endeavor, nor did he want it to be. Communism was not easy, but it was right. His ancestors had instilled this in him, and history had shown that a communist dictatorship would not fail like the weak democracy currently in place. This country was desperate for change; civil unrest was at an all-time high with the left and right clashing over virtually every policy and stance imaginable. Imagine living in a utopia where your beliefs are dictated to you, and deviating from them is punishable by the death of you or your family members. Popov sipped a yardstick filled with hurricane, a popular New Orleans cocktail, considering this prospect

37

with a widening gum-forward grin. Though extremely slight in stature, Popov more than made up for it in cunningness and drunkenness. Nothing made a diminutive man feel more powerful and in control than the drink. This situation was no different. He rubbed his balding, jaundiced head purposefully, staring deep into Hisan's eyes.

"Let me show you something, my son," Popov said as he led Hisan to a storage shed in a remote end of the abandoned lot.

He struggled to unlock the enormous padlock that had been installed on the door, as cries and moaning emanated loudly from the shed. Hisan wondered how the shed had not been investigated due to the upsetting noises coming from within. He considered the potential of this being a normal occurrence at Cracker Barrels across the country. The sound of pain and remorse were consistent with the happenings inside the restaurant itself. Eating from a trough was trying on the human digestive system, but it was the preferred way to consume breakfast with the family at Cracker Barrel. It was possible that whatever was living in this shed was somehow less miserable than the clientele only a hundred or so feet away. The structure was perfectly camouflaged by the inordinate amount of recreational vehicles in the parking lot and the sound of someone inside choking to death on their fourth plate of dry flapjacks.

They entered the shed, which was far more expansive on the inside than it appeared on the outside. It smelled as though whatever was in here had been existing exclusively on goat cheese and was noticeably lactose intolerant. The dense fog did not help matters. Hisan wasn't sure if the fog was a visible manifestation of the odor or a heinous mist created by what appeared to be a neglected essential oil diffuser. The scent of shit and lavender forcibly entered his nostrils and immediately flavored his postnasal drip. Popov instantly retched into a rusted bucket that looked like it had held the throw up of several other people who had cared to enter this godforsaken addition to an otherwise family-friendly establishment.

"You need?" he asked Hisan, pushing the bucket into his chest with the vomit spilling over the edges.

Hisan politely declined and placed the bucket back onto the rusty nails lining the floor. Popov lead him through a beaded door, colored like a Jamaican flag, which was similar to the entry of a video store's designated pornography section. Three cages were firmly installed inside the facility - in the pitch-blackness, each appeared empty at first glance. Popov tugged the chain on a loose lightbulb without a fixture and the room illuminated. A man lie apparently sleeping in each cage.

"Impressive...several grown men locked in cages, but what does it all mean?" Hisan asked Popov, scanning the cages in pure wonder.

"There was something special at the last operation," Popov responded, attempting to stroke a nonexistent chin, which was little more than just a small carbuncle that sat on his neck. "I allowed you to be seen, wanted you to be seen at that piece of crap water park! Noah's Ark was the perfect place to unveil you to our shared enemy."

"What! How could you? We operate in the shadows!" Hisan yelled, grabbing Popov by the neck and pushing him up against the cage.

"It was for one man to see you," Popov replied calmly. "Duke Dasher."

Hisan lowered him, looking deeply disturbed. Memories from that fateful evening washed over him. He recalled his precious horses, all slaughtered by Duke Dasher's negligence and his awful idea to release the domesticated mini horse hybrids into the dangers of the desert wilderness.

"They would rather die standing than live on their knees," Hisan said, turning swiftly and punching a hole through the concrete wall in front of him.

"These men have been created to help you, to help us defeat the only thing standing between us and overthrowing this government," Popov continued as he lit the wrong end of his cigarette and promptly smoked through the filter. "We had to draw Dasher out, don't you see? Get him enraged; shake his confidence in the false god he worships."

"Isn't it too soon? Plus, how can the actions of a single man, who has no actual authority, determine if an entire

40

government falls?" Hisan asked, realizing that perhaps Popov overvalued the significance of a single, devout Christian.

"Dasher represents everything this country stands for and physically, even at his older age, he still represents the only threat to you Hisan," replied Popov. Now, let me show you your new family members."

Popov rammed a cattle prod in the cage, awakening the beast inside who seemed indifferent to the shock. The creature stirred and rose, though only on all fours, as though it were part wolf or part gimp. The man, if you could call it that, looked wild-eyed at his master, thirsty to please.

"This here is Addison Beach, former Green Beret. He was kidnapped and reprogrammed both physically and mentally. His skin has been infused with a poison that, when touched or scratched, causes almost instantaneous paralysis. He represents the Egyptian plague that poisoned the livestock, crippling the Egyptian empire," Popov said, proud of his creation.

A whirring sound suddenly became audible and a hidden platform holding a slumbering Cracker Barrel patron emerged from the floor. Beach calmly walked over to the slumbering customer, who routinely passed out at the restaurant after a healthy gorge and with a prick from his finger, the animal fainted. He began convulsing and seconds later, both eyes popped out and blood sprayed freely from mouth and anus just before he finally imploded

41

in on himself. The sound of skin crumpling like loose-leaf paper made Hisan sick. Popov looked on with delight as he continued down the line of sadistic cages.

The next cage appeared empty, even in the light. Hisan stood there, confused, and wondered if what was in the cage had somehow escaped and settled down for an equally miserable life with whatever other trash lived in this god-awful city. Popov threw a piece of sirloin he had found in the garbage remnants of the Cracker Barrel into the cage. Hisan looked on, frozen by the strangeness of the situation. The slab of meat taunted Hisan, tainted and covered in asbestos or not, Popov had never offered Hisan a solid meal.

The steak disappeared as fast as he threw it down and was followed by a horrible slurping noise. Yet, it was somehow not the fastest Hisan had ever seen someone slurp up a piece of abused sirloin meat at the restaurant.

"Camouflage," Popov muttered casually.

He went on to explain the science behind modifying the former Navy Seal, Titus Rains, whose skin appeared invisible to the naked eye. This represented the darkness plague, according to Popov, who was beginning to seem equally obsessed with the Bible as Dasher was.

"This last one, you are going to love my child," Popov continued as he staggered towards the final cage.

The last cage held a man dressed in a Best Buy Geek Squad uniform. The man seemed sicker than the other abominations introduced ahead of him, pear-shaped, with skin that appeared as delicate and fragile as the dwindling sinuses of a coke fiend and just as eager to bleed. He was wearing a pair of piss-soaked khaki pants, complete with incredibly used cell phone holster, and reeked of dander. The source of the smell was explained by the unrelenting amount of flakes on the shoulders and back of his shirt. The enormous white flecks almost made the shirt appear tie-dyed; nuggets of dried flesh seemingly sewn into the very fibers of the Best Buy uniform. Hisan wondered how one man could produce that much dead skin and how someone's hair could appear simultaneously full and sparse. The seemingly endless amount of thinning strands molted out of his head like a clutching fist pulverizing week old Panda Express Chow mein. Each inflamed follicle root appearing more painful than the last. A honeycomb of chrysalises birthing and dying onto tenderized neck meat. Dried bundles of veins and nerves disintegrating through the gaping holes where healthy hair once grew like salt crumbling down the wrinkled elbow of someone named Salt Bae. The hair appeared nonexistent at times, but in the right light, and with the right wind, you could catch glimpses of it like a quivering cobweb enduring a horrific passing of gas on the way to the toilet for something more satisfying. Hisan stared at the man for what seemed like an eternity. What could this man possibly represent? Other than a sickening glimpse into Middle America, which clearly needed their help more than ever.

Something else appeared vaguely familiar about this very mentally and physically unwell looking man, but Hisan could not quite put his finger on it.

"This here is Joel Oscreen, the prominent television evangelist. He actually came here of his own free will," Popov said with a sinister smile, knowing exactly what was running through Hisan's head. "And he will kill Dasher's firstborn, the final and most powerful plague." Even Hisan marveled at the genius of the plan - using what Dasher loved most against him.

"Tonight, you will all head to rural Illinois to set our plan into motion. Dasher will pay for everything he did, and the broken shell of a man that remains will be left to watch his country transform into a blossoming communist dictatorship," continued Popov, smoking the rest of the filter on his cigarette and taking a pull from his handle of vodka, spilling most of it onto the front of his already soaked shirt.

4 Carnage in Rockford Illinois

Washington D.C,
United States

On the Blackhawk helicopter ride to Washington D.C., Dasher spent the entire flight streaming *The Passion of the Christ* on his iPhone. Though the film itself technically qualified as part of the New Testament narrative, Mel Gibson was his favorite director and it was not some Millennial bullshit movie about social injustice. It was a movie about a man giving his life for a world that did not deserve him, which he routinely fantasized about. There were also surprisingly few R-rated live-action biblical movies to be consumed, which was fine with Dasher, who preferred the written word regardless.

The existence of Hollywood and the state of California had infuriated Dasher from the moment he discovered it existed. He remembered being 31 years old and attempting to become the next pope by getting a degree from the University of Phoenix online. One of the required electives was geography and he was finally unfortunate enough to learn of the state's existence. He sat at his computer, reading page after page about the detestable state. When he concluded his research, he unloaded an entire clip into the computer monitor at the library. Several patrons looked up from their computers, but when he explained he was a papal candidate studying at the University of Phoenix, they returned to their respective pornography viewing. California was mass-producing the type of whimpering coward he despised. Godless dregs who measured success by the amount of kale they consumed or, even worse, the amount of marijuana they smoked, or

46

even worse than that, the amount of reusable straws they owned. A modern-day Sodom and Gomorrah, except with more whining and less motivation. Though Dasher had vowed to protect the country in its entirety, he sometimes resented the spirit of California and its woke residents.

After landing at the White House, Dasher immediately informed the President of several holes he noticed in the security detail. For instance, one of the guards was incompetent enough to have not tucked his pants into his standard-issue boots. More importantly than the security deficiencies was his quest to get condoms placed on the banned substances list. Dasher immediately took the opportunity to begin explaining the dangers of contraceptives to the President, who politely nodded.

"Dasher, glad you decided to come out of retirement. Can I get you anything to drink?" said President Alphonso Knudson, a man who made extremely obese, former President Taft look downright slight.

"That decision was made for me sir when the people in this world forgot how awesome God is and coffee, black as you can make it," Dasher replied, grinding his teeth. "The only thing I hate more than a terrorist is a weak cup of coffee," Dasher continued lamely as the president handed him his cup of coffee with a perplexed look plastered on his bulging face.

"Well, we'll tell you what we got so far…" began the President.

"Let me stop you right there sir. I know who this sick piece of human garbage is. Remember Operation Diesel Fist?" interrupted Dasher.

"How could I forget? On a quiet night, I can still hear the screams of those human-horse hybrids being slaughtered," replied the President, who was overcome with a visible shiver at the thought of how things unfolded all those years ago.

"That's good to hear, I remember the success of the mission as well. Anyways, the man seen at the waterpark in Wisconsin Dells was none other than the scientist that escaped my grasp all of those years ago, except he is different. He's now huge, powerful, and extremely fast, maybe faster than me." said Dasher, completely disregarding the clearly uncomfortable tone of the President.

"Look Dasher, I don't know who the hell this guy is, but you better damn well take care of it. We are struggling to keep order as is. The market has crashed and our borders are piss poor at best," replied the President.

"I realize that sir. Well, I realize the latter; those who are foolish enough to invest in the stock market deserve to lose their asses. My money is all in Red Box machine franchises and a solid gold bust of President Reagan," said Dasher proudly.

"Take a look at these Dasher. This is a 2009 Honda Civic convertible with what appears to be three men in it, though there is a fourth seat with the seat belt buckled," continued the President, producing a series of photographs and handing them to Dasher.

Dasher looked at the photograph and recognized the scientist again immediately. He quickly imagined his H3 Hummer steamrolling the Civic, crushing the three men inside, then doing donuts in a capacity crowd of motorsports fans. Foreign cars didn't deserve the honor of touching American soil. He thanked God for his imagination and the existence of the monster truck Gravedigger and readdressed the President. The President had been watching the wandering eyes of Dasher for the entirety of the thirty-second fantasy, snapping in front of his face several times and receiving no response.

"Sir that is him, but I've never seen anyone else in this car. Where was this taken?" asked Dasher, just before he ate all three of the photographs.

"Dasher, I didn't want to say anything, but now is as good of a time as any. They were last seen at a NASA-themed strip club called Moon Tits in Northern Indiana," replied the President, who didn't dare ask why Dasher had grabbed and swallowed the three substantially sized photographs. He simply watched Dasher's teeth grating and drool-soaked picture pieces spewing from the sides of his frowning mouth.

Dasher spit the remnants in his mouth onto the carpet and looked up in horror. Though the general science behind space and the unnecessary exploration of anywhere outside of the United States was definitively unpatriotic, the thought of men watching women strip nearly made Dasher boot his lunch right in front of the President. Men who didn't know a damn thing about actual living. Soulless beige sacks drinking overpriced glasses of milk while watching comparable sinners writhe around on stage to rap music - a genre that is almost too obvious to mention in Dasher's infinitely long list of culture and art that had been condemned by himself, as an extension of the Lord, as unfit for humanity.

"Apparently, the club buys decommissioned space suits and cuts the crotch out to make them sexy," explained the President, trying to break another drought of complete silence.

"Dasher?" The President said after another excruciating six minutes of silence and Dasher staring blankly over his shoulder.

"Sorry," said Dasher. "I was just fantasizing about the rapture."

The President nodded, but purely out of instinct. An altogether involuntary motion ignited by confusion and vague concern for the man sitting in front of him daydreaming about half the world being immediately taken to heaven while the remaining were left to die alone. A Hail Mary reaction to appease Dasher and with any luck propel him out of the conversation as quickly as possible. Just then, an aid walked into the room and whispered something in the President's ear.

"Dasher, the car was just spotted entering the state of Illinois," the President said, but Dasher was already gone by the time he finished the sentence.

Wind sprinting to the Blackhawk helicopter that had just dropped him off moments earlier, Dasher knew immediately that this crew of heathens was heading right for his family. Targeting the only thing Dasher cared about outside of God, his country, and servicemen and women everywhere. Dasher's standard-issue military boots pounded the pavement; his Christian themed dry-fit shirt, which read, "I stand for my flag, I kneel for my God," was drenched in sweat. The pilot exited the helicopter immediately, knowing that a far more powerful man needed the bird.

"You did the right thing," said Dasher, blasting the helicopter off the ground at a downright unsafe speed. The pilot saluted, praying that Dasher had some vague idea of how to fly.

**Somewhere in Illinois,
United States**

A Honda Civic containing four circus freaks rolled along en route to their first mission together. To kill Duke Dasher's firstborn and only child, and thus set into motion something that would change the world forever. The ride had been unimaginably uncomfortable and Hisan wondered why Popov had chosen the fun-sized Honda Civic as the ideal mode of transportation for four elite super soldiers. He surmised it was likely the 2008 JD

Power Award for compact cars, as well as the impressive highway gas mileage. Though, then again, maybe Popov had just been blackout drunk on Sutter Home minis at the car dealership and thought he was buying something more substantial.

Both scenarios were entirely in the realm of possibility. Popov loved haggling, and those he haggled with loved it even more. He would often leave the house with a 5th of Smirnoff Raspberry in hand, confident that the liquor would make the salesman more pliable. Vladimir would then return home several hours later, piss drunk with an empty 5th, having paid double for his desired item and driven home well over the legal limit. Whatever he bought was then paraded around as proof he had humiliated the salesperson completely, beaten them at their own game. He would say he had stolen something from them they would never get back, and though it was assumed he was referring to pride, in reality, it was the several hours the salesperson had spent attempting to escort an incoherent drunk who whipped his hog out of the open fly on his JNCO jeans from the premises.

The men sat in pure silence, focusing wholly on the mission at hand as it had been laid out to them. Though each of the men released from the cage was unsettling in their own right, all of them feared the man in the soiled Best Buy employee shirt. The television pastor Joel Oscreen, who had willingly locked himself inside of the depraved Cracker Barrel sister facility, seemed capable of anything. He sat with an idiotic grin on his face staring forward. His eyes never blinked and his pants were routinely re-soiled. The others in the car had been brainwashed, their minds had been stripped and reprogrammed, but this pastor wanted it. He looked at home in the packed car, sitting with both hands on his lap, motionless for the entire drive, his face an unmoving pillar of contentment and focus. Hisan had advised Addison Beach to put his hand in front of Oscreen's mouth to see if he was still breathing at specific points during the lengthy road trip, though the eye-stinging morning breath that dominated the car all but confirmed the suspicion that he was alive and unwell.

The plan was simple, according to Popov. The newly converted Joel Oscreen would pose as a member of the highly trusted Best Buy home electronics help service, Geek Squad. He would infiltrate the Dasher house and execute Terry Dasher with a sling and a stone. Though the David and Goliath parallel was a stretch at best - as this was a helpless child and not a superhuman menace hell-bent on destroying a city - Popov knew that the symbolism would not be lost on someone as devout as Dasher. Popov would convince Dasher that his God had betrayed him one way or another. He would make him turn against the book he loved, the God he loved, and break him down enough to eventually convert him into a proud communist soldier. Once converted, it would make toppling the government a breeze for Popov and the rest of his associates that already recognized the torrid political climate.

Did Popov know the depth of Dasher's love for the Lord? Did he actually think the unbreakable machine who had personally murdered dozens of Popov's former colleagues and associates would bend the knee to communism and the fall of America? He was not sure, but he would find out soon enough.

Rockford,
Illinois,
United States

The helicopter crashed to the ground in Dasher's front yard. The propeller plunged into the perfectly manicured Perennial Ryegrass as blades of grass sprayed into the air and Dasher tried desperately to catch them. Remembering that his wife and child were in imminent danger, he made the ultimate sacrifice and tossed the grass to the ground. The concern for his yard momentarily receding as he prayed he had made it home before the ruthless mercenaries arrived. Dasher knew these men were merely heavily lubricated cogs in a more giant fuck machine, but he couldn't figure out who was grinding the organ to make the animatronic mouth of the machine suck and tug anything or anyone who was unfortunate enough to grant the yearning abomination a glance. Solving that oddly paralleled sexual metaphor would have to wait. As he exited the helicopter and walked to the door, he knew something was amiss. He could almost smell it.

He drew his standard-issue military Glock and approached the house with impressive tactical precision. The door was slightly ajar, which was not abnormal; as Dasher would

54

often leave it open to tempt neighbors and criminals alike to enter his house without an explicit invitation. Several times a neighbor had knocked politely and opened the door to see if anyone was home and if everything was alright, only to see a fully nude Dasher performing the Stations of the Cross in his living room before being promptly drawn down by Dasher's standard-issue military Glock. The unfortunate ones were captured and forced to participate as Pontius Pilate in Dasher's lonely rendition of the Stations of the Cross.

The thing that threw Dasher off was it was October, which meant Christmas decorations should have gone up the day before. This was standard fare at the Dasher household in order to combat the evils brought on by Halloween. Instead of candy, the Dasher household would offer prayer cards and advice on being celibate. It was never too early to deprive yourself of joy in life according to Dasher. The prayer cards and advice on sex were politely ignored, but when it came time for the anti-abortion diatribes, the parents generally came and retrieved their confused child, then hurried them along to the next house. The amount of Halloween visitors had dwindled since the tradition became the norm several years back.

Dasher entered his house.

"Duke!" Dasher's wife yelled from the back room. "It's Terry! They've done something to Terry!"

Dasher noticed they had handcuffed his wife to the stove. She sat on her knees attempting to pry the cuffs loose from handle of the stove.

"Honey! Are you alright?" Dasher asked, his eyes darting around the room, assessing any potential risks.

"Yes, I'm unharmed, but Terry, they did something to Terry!" Stacy screamed back, shaking her wrist against the stove handle that imprisoned her.

Dasher shot the handcuffs off from across the room, not realizing that a bullet whizzing by his wife's head and the shattering of the restraints and glass front of the stove would ultimately make her more upset. She lay crying on the floor as Dasher coolly blew the smoke from his gun.

"I'm on it," Dasher said, already sprinting upstairs. His wife attempted to explain what was going on, but Dasher had already raced out of the kitchen on the way to Terry's room.

Empty.

He looked out his son's window and noticed something peculiar in the backyard. Terry stood outside with what appeared to be Joel Oscreen wearing a Best Buy Geek Squad uniform. Dasher rubbed his eyes, trying to make sense of what the hell was going on. He fired several shots through the window in the general vicinity of whoever this stranger was. Best Buy employee or not, you do not handcuff a man's wife to the stove.

Moreover, you sure as hell don't try to look like celebrity pastor, Joel Oscreen. Dasher spent countless weekends and anniversary dinners outlining his mistrust for both the internet and anyone who worked as a Best Buy Geek Squad employee, but clearly, Stacy hadn't listened to either of the paranoid thoughts. The latter concerned Stacy slightly, as the employees of a dying big box technology store were generally benign. Nobody ever listened to Duke, yet he was always right. Dasher climbed calmly out of the window and walked towards the happening in the backyard.

"Hello Duke," said the man in the Best Buy uniform. Dasher immediately recognized the voice.

He had listened to it during thousands of televised prayer services. It was the unmistakably shrill, hissing voice of one of the few men worthy of getting into heaven - Joel Oscreen.

"Joel! What is going on here? Why are you wearing a Best Buy uniform? Why did you chain my wife to the stove and why are you holding a sling and a rock aimed at my son?" Dasher said, his mind trying to process the contradictory behavior of his beloved television pastor.

"The Best Buy uniform got me into your house in the first place Dasher. Don't you realize that without it, your wife would have never let me in? She hates me Dasher. She always has. However, by convincing her I had fallen on hard times and was now trying to make an honest living doing home electronic repairs, her Christian heart was unable to resist lending a helping hand and letting me in," said Oscreen.

The explanation didn't make a lot of sense and Dasher thought it more likely that Oscreen was just fulfilling an odd fantasy about a Best Buy employee home invasion.

"You're lying Joel," said Dasher. "Tell me you're here to perform my yearly baptism," he continued. Dasher got baptized every year for good measure, often telling people he generally got it done after his prostate exam. "Kill two birds with the same stone!" he would say, leaving people to wonder how the seemingly disparate rituals could be done at the same time by the same person in the same profession.

"Dasher, I'm here to kill your first-born son. This sling and this rock will crush the boy's head in the same fashion Goliath fell to David," replied Oscreen.

At that very minute, and not a moment before, Dasher realized Joel Oscreen was there to kill his first-born son. On the one hand, he respected it. Oscreen was carrying out a by-the-books, tried and true Old Testament execution. But now, the rites of the good ole days, where millions of people were hastily judged and then died by the hand of a righteous, omnipotent being were being acted upon his son. Dasher could comprehend transforming entire city populations into salt and destruction of most of the earth via flood, but God would have never instructed this pastor to murder his son. Dasher would not let his son suffer the same fate as Goliath. His son would not become an Old Testament punchline, not on his watch.

"Joel, put down the sling; we can talk this through, just as two God-fearing men should," said Dasher, who, in any other circumstance would have killed the hostage and the threat, but because this was a celebrity pastor holding his son hostage, he waded cautiously towards a peaceful resolution.

He knew that whatever had happened to Joel Oscreen, some good still had to exist in there. Even though the pastor was a little new wave for Dasher and very slightly leaned on New Testament teachings, which had spawned an insufferable generation of Millennials, he still respected the hell out of someone who had made God that popular. It was something he had tried for years to do, but his abrasive nature and unwillingness to accept anything that was not literal interpretations of the written word had made him polarizing. Nevertheless, absolutely no one was better at worshipping God than Dasher. Furthermore, no one was better at protecting the United States.

Oscreen swung the sling seductively, staring deep into Dasher's soul. Terry Dasher had since disappeared from the bizarre biblical confrontation, which appeared somewhat sexual to on looking neighbors, between two grown men in a backyard in rural Illinois.

"Your move Dasher. I know you're incapable of killing me. At least that's what Popov was betting on," Oscreen said, as a stain slowly grew in his already blemished, pleated khaki pants.

Popov. Dasher had heard that name before. But where? He frantically searched through the desolate wasteland of blind faith and irrational judgments that filled his enormous skull. Popov, he thought, as he began sprinting towards Oscreen, who he would subdue, water board and convert back to real Christianity - an act that even he shuddered at in terms of its impressiveness. Most of the souls he had saved via brute force were in no way as influential as Oscreen. A conversion of this magnitude would be an enormous resume builder on his bid for heaven. He even imagined God endorsing him on LinkedIn for 'Best Conversion Ever', which would go perfectly with his only other endorsement for 'Networking'. Heck, maybe it would become a CBS sitcom at some point and his son Terry could play him. Then he considered the prospect of Terry becoming something as despicable as an actor and immediately cast the thought from his head.

As he began to run, everything went black. He felt two hands touch his eyes and then the whole world went black. Two hands, which felt like saliva-covered corncobs and reeked of unscented Vaseline. The next thing he knew, he was being dragged across the yard by several men. He lay motionless; he knew that without his vision, there was no chance of fighting off four tactically trained soldiers. One or two, maybe, but not four. Though otherwise wholly still, he loudly prayed through several decades of his mental rosary. Dasher learned this in the military as a time tracking mechanism, which in turn allowed him to measure the distance he traveled. Some used the sun; Dasher used prayer, which given his current physical status, he was thankful. The prayers boomed and echoed through the neighborhood and made the neighbors' eardrums quiver. In an attempt to shut Dasher up, the four mercenaries took turns raining blows down on him as he lay helpless, but no one can shut up God. The fists only served to increase the volume of Dasher's prayers, which, by the time they reached the car, had escalated into just a single unsettling brown note flowing from Dasher's agape mouth. Dasher had once told Stacy and Terry Dasher that if singing is like praying twice as hard, deafening, incomprehensible screaming is like praying three times even that. Volume is ultimately the deciding factor in how authentic a prayer is, this was written in a little known scripture by a little known thirteenth apostle who looked like the bastard cousin of Bartholomew.

Dasher counted the paces through prayer on the way to the trunk of the Honda Civic he was thrown into. He instantly recognized it as a Civic because of the tiny trunk space and what he deemed to be shoddy craftsmanship. He could always identify a foreign-made product, something intangibly inferior to those built in the confines of the United States borders. The thought of being stuffed into the trunk of anything that didn't have towing capacity only served to infuriate him further. He laid and waited in the back; he knew whatever lie ahead would test every conviction he ever had. These men wanted to break him, that much was certain.

5 Contraceptives Finally Used for Good

Route 66 to California,
United States

The four men looked at each other, knowing they just captured something more valuable than any religious artifact ever, and did it with relative ease for that matter. Joel Oscreen sat in the backseat in total silence once again. The other mercenaries suffered through the outcome of the intense standoff that manifested in his khaki pants. A cement snake was seemingly working its way through his intestines and producing more noxious gas than previously thought possible. Hisan had offered to pull over at a rest area for relief, but Oscreen declined immediately, claiming he and the snake within would never be separated. Everyone began calculating in their head how long it could have been since his last bowel movement. The car smelled like a sickly cat pissing blood into an onion volcano on a white-hot hibachi grill. Whatever Oscreen had eaten in the weeks prior had turned his intestines into dust.

The other three members fought to keep down the Arby's Big Montana sandwiches they had treated themselves to at the last rest stop. The heaving fistfuls of meat were becoming difficult to digest in the stench of the car. They were not out of the clear yet though; they still had one of the most dangerous men in the world shoved in the trunk of a car that still had a long way to go to get to the interrogation location Popov had meticulously set: Los Angeles, California. A place Dasher had routinely dismantled in the comments section of Infowars.com and had publicly condemned during a rather peculiar speech given at a charity event for Mothers Against Drunk

Driving several years prior to the kidnapping. Though the speech was barely relevant and filled to the brim with factual inaccuracies, he had received a standing ovation.

Los Angeles would be the perfect setting to destroy Dasher's will.

Something about the situation was not sitting right for Hisan though and it wasn't just the roast beef log from Arby's. The 60/40 ground beef blend was waging trench warfare in every fold of his stomach lining. The gristle bayonets sticking and driving into his already deteriorating innards. Dasher was known for his preparedness. He was known for his ruthlessness. Many enemies knew him as God Hand, as his methods of careless destruction were comparable to the deity described in the Bible he carried everywhere. He had seemed vulnerable in this confrontation. Soft.

Given Dasher's age and his time away from the military, maybe he had lost a step, thought Hisan. He had left himself completely vulnerable, but why? The poison from Addison Beach's hands had successfully blinded him, but the thought of Dasher allowing someone to sneak up behind him perplexed Hisan. It was entirely possible that Dasher was as mediocre and dull as every other bootlicking loser in the cul de sac, who were in similarly sexless marriages with kids they resented. He turned around and eyed the trunk wearily, wishing he hadn't left Dasher alone and unseen in the confines of a Honda Civic trunk.

Route 66 to California,
Honda Civic Trunk,
United States

Dasher lay calmly in the back of the piece of crap Honda Civic. "Reliability my ass," thought Dasher, who ten years earlier had spit hot coffee in the face of a sales representative when he offered to put him in an affordable and reliable Honda model. Afterwards, Dasher had lamely offered an almost unintelligible apology. Though he would never intentionally hurt someone who was not an enemy of the country, he couldn't be certain someone like this wasn't. In Dasher's mind, anyone willing to sell foreign cars certainly had the potential to turn on the country at a moment's notice, and this salesperson was no different. He offered the man cash and did no negotiating for the car he drove now - a beautiful Chevy Silverado - the thought of which prompted Dasher to fantasize about the spacious trunk he knew and loved.

His plan had worked perfectly. There was no progress being made on the attacks happening across the country, and with no real leads about where they would strike next, Dasher knew by being the sacrificial lamb, he could put himself in the crosshairs of these lunatics, thus briefly saving the American public from additional attacks led by one of the men who kidnapped him. He could care less about his life; he only served his country, his family, and his God. All he longed for was a safe, pure, God-fearing existence for his loved ones, the abolition of the Democratic Party, and the eradication of all contraceptives. Was that so much to ask for in this world?

He did not anticipate being blinded by the mere hands of someone who grabbed him from behind, or the lengthy standoff with celebrity pastor Joel Oscreen, who seemed utterly unglued and was inexplicably wearing an extremely soiled Best Buy uniform. A pastor who spent decades preaching the good of God turning out to be some sick bastard was unheard of. Who had gotten to him? Why did he turn? What was his obsession with murdering Terry Dasher and more importantly, Best Buy? Duke was still uncertain what the endgame was, but he knew he had a hidden tactical advantage. Soon enough, they would all be blind. Dasher began slowly rolling his tongue - working something out of his stomach he assumed he would never have to use.

He thought the object buried underneath stomach acid, bile, and a lifetime of regret mixed with Eucharist wafers would never need to be unearthed. He could feel the tinge of the string coming from the back of his throat as his tongue continued punching forward, working on getting his final lifeline from the depths of his ulcer-ridden stomach. Finally, he caught the string in his teeth and spit what appeared to be a bloody phlegm sack onto the floor of the trunk.

The gelatinous abscess shined in the dog hair-covered trunk. A condom filled with what was described to him as the blood of Judas and the complimentary matchbook that had come with it. A decade ago, Dasher and his wife had visited the Vatican, a trip that narrowly topped their honeymoon at Universal Studios Orlando. He asked a gift shop employee where the real religious artifacts were, slyly

66

palming the acne-covered burnout a crisp two-dollar bill with a wink and a smile. In any other circumstance, Dasher wouldn't have engaged in something as unsavory as bribery, but this was the Vatican, and his thirst for a memorable souvenir was unstoppable. There was also the assumption that God would undeniably want him to be a protector of something that was considered sacred by a group of drooling geriatrics, who preached intolerance while flogging non-believers with solid gold shepherd's staffs and climaxing into frankincense-drenched decorative hats while torturing churchgoers with brutally conceived jokes.

After several hours of badgering, the employee came back with what appeared to be a blood-filled condom and described it as having been extracted from Judas right before he died of auto-erotic-asphyxiation. The legend of Judas passing from AEA was widely disputed at varying Christian gatherings and summits. Dasher was always under the belief that was the only way a coward like that would go. Dasher seemed skeptical of the relic at first, but using a condom to transport precious material made sense given the fact that using it any other way was a sin. He picked up the slippery latex pouch and pondered it; though the relic was from someone considered evil by Christians, Dasher figured the strength and spirituality he wielded in his body would be the perfect residence for the vile liquid.

He had offered the gift shop employee one hundred dollars for the bulging sack that seemed like it could burst at any moment. The supposed relic from ancient times. The fact that the remnant was from the New Testament was unfortunate, but a tourist gift shop like this would never be selling something so coveted from the Old Testament, so Dasher settled. Stacy tugged on Dasher's sleeve and quietly suggested there was a slight possibility that the blood was not as ancient and holy as advertised. Dasher listened carefully to Stacy and rubbed his chin, considering her warning. Ultimately, he put the money on the counter, his desire for belief smothering any rational thought. The gift shop employee seemed satisfied, albeit confused by the offer and the audible monologue from Dasher as he aggressively debated the purchase with himself. Stacy almost prevented the sale with her reasonable skepticism, but when the employee produced a soiled piece of loose-leaf paper with an official endorsement written in number two pencil from Pope John Paul IV, Dasher knew it was a genuine artifact. He spent the rest of the trip determining what to do with the newly acquired object before ultimately deciding to swallow it. Save it for a rainy day, he told his confused looking wife with a warm smile. Stacy smiled and nodded, but she wondered what rainy day activity could possibly warrant using this mysterious and questionable relic.

Dasher was not sure what he meant by the cryptic statement either; he just had an intuition that the holy item would come in handy someday, and that day was today. Though he would have preferred not to destroy something so sacred on something as frivolous as saving his own life, he knew the country needed him, so his coveted souvenir would meet the same fate as the person it was extracted from. He bit into the threadbare latex, immediately sensing the chemical metallic taste that accompanies ancient blood that has been sitting in a condom inside a stomach for several years. He sprayed the blood on every inch of the trunk he could.

Dasher thought back on his interaction with the souvenir shop salesmen who said the book of matches paired perfectly with the relic. At the time, it seemed strange. He wasn't sure what to make of it but he knew the two items must never be separated. Now looking back, he fully believed that the gift shop employee had been a guardian angel sent by God himself, knowing that Dasher would find himself in this exact situation. He had been provided the blood of the ultimate betrayer, which legend has it, was so vile and evil, it was in fact flammable. A match was struck between his teeth and the trunk illuminated; Dasher's smile exceeded the boundaries of his face, his eyes hypnotized by the flame.

Dasher thought about the irony of a contraceptive finally being used for good instead of evil -giving life instead of taking it away. Dasher was the happiest he had been in years.

Route 66 to California,
Honda Civic Trunk,
United States

Titus Rains immediately smelled the smoke in the back of the Honda Civic. As he turned around, he saw the trunk was fully engulfed in flames. Just as soon as he noticed the fire, a bald and horribly burned Dasher had birthed through the center console divider in the back of the Civic.

Several hunks of charred skin toppled onto the floor of the Civic, like a carving station at Fogo de Chão. His eyes were ghostly white from the poison Addison Beach had administered during the confrontation several hours earlier.

Dasher's mouth was covered in blood. Rains had no idea where it was from, but the gnashing teeth appeared eager for more human flesh and the insatiable taste of revenge. Several other passing cars on the highway looked on in terror; they would struggle to digest the moment for the rest of their lives. Decades of therapy would not pacify the brutal post-traumatic stress that accompanies watching a blind man chew off the hands of another man in a flaming Honda Civic. Dasher immediately felt the flesh in his teeth; his only concern was choking on the fingers as the bones snapped clean off. Fortunately, he swallowed the fingers with relative ease. This wasn't the first time he had chewed a man's fingers off, and it certainly wouldn't be the last.

Hisan turned around to see Titus Rains holding up his severely mauled hand and screeching like a burlap sack full of rats being drowned to make a fresh batch of knuckle steaks for carnival night at a Ponderosa in Northern Indiana. Hisan had taken his eyes off the road, a mistake that would cost him dearly. The blood spraying from Rains' hand also served to blind Hisan. By the time he turned back around, the Honda Civic was careening towards the shoulder of the road. The car launched off a cement barrier and into a barrel roll. It hit the ground, and once again, everything went black

6 The Betrayal of Duke Dasher

Washington D.C.,
United States

President Knudson sat in the custom-made chair that had been made for a man of his stature. Even with the custom chair, the springs pleaded for mercy as Knudson adjusted himself in a perpetual war to find comfort. He had been battling a case of athlete's foot on his ass for months, and each adjustment in the chair reopened another barely healed blister. The President's doctors advised him to avoid any itching, but the President scooted furiously in his chair - the relief provided by the friction on the ergonomically correct seat was almost orgasmic. So despite warnings from doctors, Knudson's flaking ass cheeks ground into the wool chair with an uncanny enthusiasm. Rocking back and forth like a splintering old row boat lost at sea, seeking and failing to find reprieve from the chapped tentacles of the Kraken that haunted his hole. The White House office itself was aggressively beige and indifferently decorated. It was a perfect representation of the current political climate in which forward momentum and progress were gleefully ignored.

President Knudson found himself, like most Americans, sitting alone in a room, suffering through a hapless existence while refreshing the Barstool Sports Twitter feed in order to euthanize actual human emotion and thought by way of GIFs and Boomerangs. He considered sadly masturbating, but instead, decided to turn on the news, which required the same mental capacity as the aforementioned activity, though it had been particularly painful to watch in recent weeks. News of continuing attacks against America was pouring in from varying parts of the country. On top of it all, Duke Dasher had disappeared. Was Dasher somehow a part of these attacks? President Knudson knew Dasher feared God, but did he fear the authority of this country? Had God turned his vengeful eye towards an America that was rapidly descending into madness?

Everyone was a suspect at this point, and Dasher's untimely disappearance was not helping his cause. Was he working with the four mercenaries the President had shown him driving towards his house? He had left rather abruptly. It was entirely possible Dasher had hijacked that helicopter as a means to wreak more havoc on a country already on its knees. The President grew more suspicious of Dasher by the minute. He turned the events repeatedly in his head, the paranoia slowly transforming Dasher into a monster capable of anything. The helicopter had been recovered at Dasher's house, where his wife and son were interviewed. The interviews had been fruitless however, as the wife described a deranged Joel Oscreen as the primary culprit, Knudson quickly dismissed her account of events given his relationship with Christianity and televised sermons. They were back at square one after leaving Dasher's wife and kid unguarded and emotionally neglected in the confines of the house they were almost killed in. Knudson had grown furious that more information could not be extracted from the two; he briefly considered waterboarding but thought better of it, mostly from fear of retribution from Dasher himself.

Fortunately for the President, the attacks were happening with such regularity that they were generally buried under the onslaught of other celebrity gossip and directionless outrage. There was a numbing cadence to the atrocities, which allowed the President to consistently offer up prayers for varying victims without the public realizing the prayers were for separate crimes against humanity. The nation was stuck in a self-imposed stalemate of sorts - seemingly seeking change, but too apathetic to exchange actual physical effort for the endless streams of content being hammered into their bleeding eye sockets. Maybe humanity had run its course. Maybe watching a stranger doing squats in white spandex was more important than anything else. Perhaps gazing at Kris Kardashian harvesting her children for organs in an effort to make a new all-natural Xanax lip filler was the most significant thing someone could do in their life. What was left in the world was pulsating legions of maggots slurping the last little bit of rotten, sagging flesh from the rapidly disintegrating corpse of humankind. Maybe the perpetual cycle of chewing and spitting up, reheating, and snorting ejaculate from varying social media content orgies was not healthy. Maybe the blue light was killing everyone faster than the men snapping necks. Knudson immediately cast the thought aside after watching another gender reveal fail on Instagram. If not this, what did we really have?

Knudson scrolled through Twitter and realized the news of the most recent attack had been buried under a story about one of the Real Housewives of Beverly Hills suffering from loose bowels. He chuckled at the coincidence that he had recently been suffering from the same affliction. The most recent attacks adhered to the prior ones inflicted on the country, happening primarily in depleted Midwestern States that ultimately helped swing the election in his favor. Each attack was as horrific as the last, with surprisingly no bullets fired, but rather dozens upon dozens of snapped necks. Families were being torn apart by this. It was only a matter of time before the celebrity gossip culture dried up, and the attacks were prioritized.

"Get Watley in here," President Knudson yelled as he wrestled a full chicken bone down his protesting throat.

Tom Watley promptly entered the Oval Office, noting an immense stench that governed every inch of the room. Watley saw the boiling red face of President Knudson and immediately recognized the look of severe indigestion and misplaced anger. He anticipated the meeting going poorly.

"President Knudson, a pleasure to finally meet you. I've heard so many good things," Watley said sheepishly, hoping that some lambasting would keep the president from shitting his pants during the meeting, which he had been rumored to do if unhappy enough.

"Tell me something Watley. You were Duke Dasher's commanding officer during the mission that forced him into retirement, were you not?" replied Knudson.

"Yes sir, that's correct. His method of cutting off the face of the leader, wearing it as a mask and convincing the rest of the terrorists to commit suicide wasn't necessarily in the

Geneva Convention, but it sure as hell got the job done. If it hadn't caused so much outrage, I would have given him a purple heart and two weeks paid vacation," said Watley.

"That's not what I'm after Watley. We are all well aware that doing that was simple American ingenuity. I know your decision to honorably discharge him was a difficult one that was highly influenced by backward leftist media. The real problem is Dasher has now been missing for weeks, and these attacks keep happening," the President replied, gnawing the last piece of a hangnail off.

The way the President had left the sentence hanging made Watley uneasy, as did the President's relentless squirming and micro belching.

"Sir, I'm not sure I follow," said Watley.

"What I'm getting at is I think Dasher might be behind these attacks," continued the President.

"Sir, you can't be serious. Dasher is fiercely loyal to this country, almost to a fault. Don't you recall the time he almost divorced his wife for accidentally forgetting to remove her hat during the national anthem of an NFL game? If divorce weren't a sin, they would no longer be together, sir. Mind you, this also occurred in their living room during a DVR'd stream of a game from a decade prior. Not to mention, he strictly abides by the concept that only sinners should be casualties of war," Watley said, staring at the carpeting and remembering the irate phone call he had received from Dasher the day of the incident.

"Watley, something stinks about this whole situation, and frankly, we are desperate to pin this on someone so we can start up a morale-boosting manhunt. Just what this country needs," the President replied, placing his hand awkwardly on Watley's knee.

"Sir, Dasher could very much so be in trouble. He may need our help," said Watley.

"He won't get it. He made that decision for himself when he decided to go dark," the President replied, leaning back in his chair and taking a hero's load from his JUUL. The plume engulfed Watley's face, which was too stunned to evade the thickness and depth of the mango scented money shot. Enormous plumes like these had been the perfect way to prove imaginary dominance, and in President Knudson's mind, Watley had just been cucked into oblivion. He ordered Watley to leave his office immediately. Watley looked at the President in disbelief before abiding by the request. He thought back to a saying that Duke had taught him during their time in the military together, *vaping hands are the devil's playground.* The phrase had seemed arbitrary at best, but now the phrase idled in Watley's mind like the smoke that followed him as he left the room. He had seen something more than just a hangover and an addiction to softcore pornography in the President's bloodshot eyes, something sinister was hatching from his popcorn lungs.

President Knudson picked up the phone and demanded an immediate press conference. Watley looked on completely perplexed, knowing that what was coming might shake the country to its very core. In a remote part of Southern Illinois, Popov listened to the entire conversation through his laptop. The $25 in Kohls Cash he had paid the janitor to plant a bug in the President's office had been money well spent. Popov got all of the information he needed and the janitor could now get a shrimp deveiner, a travel sized lava lamp, a pair of potentially used Nikes and Burn Notice Season 3 on Blu Ray from an iconic department store. The government was imploding on itself, just as Popov had predicted. Now if he could just get a hold of Hisan and the three other mercenaries with their precious cargo.

Somewhere in Montana, United States

When Hisan awoke, he was upside down. His head was pounding. He unbuckled his seatbelt and crawled from the overturned Honda Civic. The three other goons stood around a small campfire they had built. How long had he been out? Moreover, why hadn't they unbuckled him and pulled him from the car? He had been left hanging upside down for a countless number of hours or days. With friends like these, who needs enemies, thought Hisan. If these had been his mini horses, they would have released him from the car immediately.

"Where are we?" Hisan demanded, recalling that the car flipped onto the shoulder of the road on a busy stretch of highway in Montana.

"We're exactly where we need to be and nowhere else," Joel Oscreen replied cryptically.

"We were at risk of being seen, so we got out and dragged the car into the woods where we believe Dasher ran off after the crash," Titus Rains added, nursing an infected looking bloody stump full of mangled fingers that Dasher had eaten up like a wood chipper.

"And you couldn't have pulled me from the car first?" asked Hisan infuriated.

The group shrugged and returned to gazing blankly into the fireplace app that one of them had downloaded onto their tablet. Hisan wondered why they hadn't started a real fire but didn't bother to ask, any eccentricities these psychopaths exhibited could be attributed to being sequestered outside of a Cracker Barrel for the better part of a decade. Dasher had somehow bested them, and though they were genetically engineered elite murderous psychopaths, they still possessed the conventional fragile masculinity that accompanied all men who are incapable of getting laid. Each of them struggled to internally justify the failure at hand. Each making excuses, overcompensating, posturing, and using irrational blame as a mechanism to cope with their own shortcomings. The judgment never turning inwards, but instead spewing outwards like the blood from Rain's gnawed off fingers. The incident had severely wounded the already delicate nature of these creatures who had been programmed exclusively for killing. Fortunately enough, when male confidence is challenged, the direct product is uncontrollable and misdirected rage. This rage would transfer straight to the hunt of Duke Dasher, who had, for now, put their perceived manhood under a microscope. A fantasy of capturing and torturing Dasher consumed them all. It would be the only way to win back their confidence and avoid a lifetime of impotence.

They each wondered how the hell he started that fire and though none would admit it, the vision of Dasher's flaming, bald head birthing through the seat was making them all very uncomfortable. Hisan approached the fire being standard definition broadcasted from the tablet. If they were going to find Dasher, they would have to split up. Unfortunately, they would have to wait until morning to continue the hunt. If they did it at night, they would be in Dasher's realm of blindness.

Dasher was undoubtedly injured in the crash and was visibly on fire right before the car turned over, so he would be alone in the woods and losing strength by the minute. If they waited it out until morning, he would be a shell of a man by the time they found him. He may even die in the woods, which would be all the same for Hisan, who thought the corpse could then be defiled and used as communist propaganda. Imagining Dasher's dead body used as a marionette during a commercial advertising the health benefits of grain alcohol satisfied Hisan to no end. Popov would be happy with Dasher dead or alive; they just needed to capture him one way or another.

Hisan laid out the plan for the other men. They would each scout a section of the woods and flush Dasher towards a clearing in the middle of the forest. He distributed firearms and flare guns to each of the members. If anyone found him, they were to shoot a flare into the air, letting the others know Dasher was being flushed to the clearing. Once in the expanse, the final confrontation could begin yet again, and the team could put this country back on the track to a communist regime installation. They gathered around the fire and prepared themselves for an undoubtedly restless sleep. The plan seemed simple enough, though nothing was simple when it came to Dasher. Even wounded, Dasher was more dangerous than most men were.

At the other end of the woods, Dasher lay under a pile of dead leaves. When the car had crashed, he propelled through the front windshield, landing a dozen or so feet from the vehicle itself. He instantly felt the beautiful 6,000-year-old planet underneath him and started crawling. He remembered being fascinated at the age of the earth; several thousand years was a very long time for a planet to exist. Once more, he thanked his guardian angel for selling him a condom full of flammable blood from the traitor Judas. He also thanked God for cursing Judas with the flammable blood, an ingenious penance for ratting out his only Son. Dasher thought it was inspiring that the Bible could still surprise him every day. Even though he had read the book thousands of times in favor of other literature, there was always something new to cherish. He would have to talk with his professor at the University of Phoenix about getting the flammable blood and autoerotic asphyxiation story officially added to the Bible. Dasher got excited about his contribution to the Bible, being immortalized in his favorite book seemed far overdue. Though Dasher was still blind, he could hear birds chirping in the distance and instantly began crawling towards them, knowing they were in the forest where he would need to seek refuge. He made it deeper into the woods and buried himself in more dead leaves to increase his camouflage until he could figure out his next move. He reached his hand into his pair of tactical cargo pants and felt the beautiful, familiar shame that accompanied feeling the fray of the worn pages contained in his Bible.

He had nothing else in terms of survival gear and could not physically read the Bible. Nonetheless, he thanked God once more for giving him the opportunity to sit in nature and plan the brutal murder of the four men who kidnapped him. God would be impressed with the cruelty Dasher anticipated employing when exacting his revenge. He focused on the light breeze brushing across his face and the smell of decomposing wood filling his blood-caked nostrils. What if this was the same forest Adam bit the forbidden fruit in? Dasher thought longingly about being the first man and easily refusing the temptation of the fruit and the knowledge it possessed. Adam could technically be considered the first iteration of a Millennial cuck: a self-indulgent asshole who obsessed over himself instead of the greater good. If he hadn't eaten that apple, we would all still be living happily without unique thought or complex emotion in the Garden of Eden and this entire debacle would have likely never happened. He cursed Adam for taking the fruit and Eve for being a woman. All of which he now saw as a catalyst for his favorite pastor attempting to murder him and having to endure an entire generation of sniveling snowflakes.

In the midst of this bizarre, beginning of humankind daydream, Dasher smelled the sickening scent of incense burning in the distance. Incense was never burned without marijuana and though severely injured and blind, Dasher longed with every fiber in his being to find the party responsible and offer a stern reprimanding.

Washington D.C., United States

President Knudson struggled up the stairs on the way to the podium, his knees nearing collapse with every pained step. They shook under his enormous stature, bowing inwards with every step forward. He reminded himself to fire the intern who was supposed to install a miniature lift up to the podium at press conferences like this. He had demanded a lift be created to make him appear more powerful, being hoisted like a god three feet off the ground to the stage where the podium stood. The makeup that had been applied made his face less human than usual. It sat squarely above his skin, making it appear as though he was wearing a lumpy, glistening Halloween mask that had been poorly sewn onto his dehydrated skin. A vast cold sore looked particularly disturbing as it feasted on the chalky makeup, making it appear like a syringe erupting with gristle-forward ground turkey. The rolling sand dunes of grainy, blemished skin seemed to stretch forever.

There was also an odd-looking contour applied to his

83

cheeks to thin them out, but it made his face resemble a deflating hunk of roadkill gasping its last few breaths of air rather than thin it. Every liver spot was its own sickly tide pool; the yellowing waters stirred visibly beneath his thinning skin, which looked ready for puncture from one of the hardened growths he referred to as his intestine barnacles. His suit was visibly drenched and the walk caused him to break into a full drop sweat. Undetermined fluids were leaking from his sweat-logged sleeves.

Nonetheless, the President took to the podium like a hero and the country watched on because they had nothing else to do. The only remote escape from their otherwise regrettable existence. Something to lap up and disgorge into the ringing ear drums of friends and family who also watched the pointless occurrence and established an equally uninteresting opinion. Something to fill the time between Hawaii 5.0, Two and a Half Men reruns and death. The President served as something to strive towards for much of the public: an overweight, overpaid public servant with eternal indigestion, uncompromising sleep apnea and a loose grasp on the English language.

"I would first like to comment on the important, recent news that one of the Real Housewives of Beverly Hills has been suffering from loose bowels. I would like to offer my sincerest thoughts and prayers in this difficult time!" Knudson said purposefully into the mic. The crowd immediately exploded in applause at the heartfelt condolences. The first of many undeserved standing ovations that would occur during the press conference.

"But what I would really like to talk to you about today is the recent attacks on our country. Sources are telling me these attacks are being fueled by none other than disgraced war veteran Duke Dasher," Knudson continued, hoping he could focus the hatred and anxiety of an entire country on a single man.

The crowd sat silently, uncertain how to react. Watley stared at the President in shock; Dasher was never described as disgraced by anyone. How could the President think this was the right thing to do?

"Bear with me," continued Knudson. He was now out of breath from talking for several seconds continuously and his right arm began to go numb. "I didn't believe it myself either, but no one has seen Dasher for weeks and these attacks are happening with increased regularity! We believe Dasher has gone rogue!" screamed the President as white flecks from his mouth covered the front row of reporters who accepted the spray with the delight of a child in the splash zone, watching an abused Orca be flogged to death at SeaWorld with commemorative mugs sold at the gift shop.

The crowd had heard enough extremely loose evidence to be satisfied. The reporters began firing questions at the President. When did he think Dasher had turned? What was the motif? How would he be stopped and was it possible to get Operation Diesel Fist removed from the history books? The President had no further comment on the incident, knowing the statement was incendiary enough to start a nationwide manhunt for Dasher. Guilty or not, this government needed a win, and capturing a scapegoat for slaughter would almost certainly guarantee another term.

However, one young reporter eyed the melting President with skepticism. The rest of the crowd were eager to be the first to break the story that a former national hero had turned on his country, but he refused to believe Dasher would change allegiance so quickly. Patrick Kibby stood in the sea of reporters carefully surveying the President's mannerisms. A former TMZ reporter, who now worked exclusively for Buzzfeed News, Kibby was well versed in sniffing out red herrings. He had a reputation for going where no one wanted to go and report on things that absolutely no one wanted to read. He once broke a story detailing the pornography preferences of Chumlee from the hit show *Pawn Stars*. Although the article managed only fourteen views, the content was interesting enough for Buzzfeed News to hire him on full-time as their new political correspondent. Kibby was the type of guy to own both a drone and a 3D printer and relentlessly talk about them. The kind of absolute loser who regularly participates in escape rooms and indoor skydiving.

Kibby maneuvered his way out of the crowded room; he had to get some air. Something seemed off with the President. Yes, it was a borderline elderly man in clearly failing health making feeble attempts to lead the most powerful country in the world, but there was something even more peculiar than that. Dasher had been at the White House only weeks earlier and had a personal meeting with the President. Kibby discovered this while documenting a new article for Buzzfeed Politics titled "*Top 10 Glory Holes You Didn't Know About Inside the Whitehouse*". What happened at that meeting? It ended with Dasher sprinting to a Blackhawk helicopter outside and taking off in a hurry. If Kibby could figure out where that Blackhawk went, he could start pulling the shit thread on this shit sweater and find out whose shit covered hands had woven the whole damn thing in a JoAnn Fabric bathroom. This was his world, wading around in the sewage and entrails from the Perdue Chicken slaughtering plant to find that golden beak. The truth amid a world of deceit.

7 An Unlikely Friendship

Somewhere in Montana,
United States

Dasher approached the scent of incense through the thick forest. He reached a clearing with a finely manicured lawn all things considered. He knew this was someone's dwelling by the feel of the grass. That someone was likely a criminal given the scent of sandalwood incense emanating through the chimney. Though the smell infuriated Dasher beyond belief, he had to admit that crawling around, blinded by chemicals on the floor of the dank forest, felt more like home than anything else had in the last decade.

The insufferable routine that accompanied suburban life had been slowly bleeding out Dasher for years. Unbeknownst to him, he was growing dull. Indeed, his religious fanaticism and immovable set of societal beliefs had kept some edge, but his survival instinct and his connection with the earth itself had withered. Wandering aimlessly in an enormous air-conditioned department store and fighting to maintain consciousness while grinning lunatics tried to shove free samples into his mouth was the most considerable discomfort he endured now. Though the wholly forgettable days came and passed, Dasher had never questioned them, as human beings really had no control over what God's plan dictated. If someone was made to be born and die with virtually no legacy and no contribution to society, than that preconceived destiny would at least provide them eternal happiness in the afterlife. Dasher was lucky though. God gave him the explicit right to defend family and country by any means necessary. He gave him the strength to murder anyone

89

who threatened either entity and blessed him with the ability to forget the atrocity all together once it was done.

He crawled for what seemed like hours, all in an effort to shame and reprimand whatever poor sap thought he could light incense on his personal property in the middle of the woods. Despite being hunted by four ruthless mercenaries, no one was exempt from condemnation in Dasher's mind. He reached what felt like a sidewalk and crawled forward. He would hit the door soon enough, and whoever was inside would get a stern talking to.

The owner of the house gazed out the window. An extremely burned, irate man appeared to be seizing his way up to the house. He recognized him instantly as Duke Dasher. He had seen his face on the news, which had been broadcasted by all of the major news networks. He was considered unstable and extremely dangerous, according to CNN. The owner of the house opened the door and receded back inside; he sat in his worn leather chair and drank his tea, waiting reluctantly for Dasher to eventually approach.

Dasher reached the front steps and called out.

"Hello! I smelled incense coming from your house. If that is to cover up the smell of marijuana you are in deep shit," said Dasher. Silence.

Dasher continued to painstakingly crawl and entered the house wondering if he had made a mistake expending this much energy in an attempt to confront someone over a misdemeanor crime. He also contemplated the idea that the mercenaries might be waiting inside the house with pillowcases full of Irish Spring soap bars, eager to bludgeon him to death. He immediately justified the choice in his head, noting that no one was exempt from God's watchful eye. If that meant his death, then so be it.

"Duke Dasher," said the shadowy figure. Dasher could smell the thick aroma of tobacco and dander in the air.

Dasher heard the voice and immediately got to his feet in a fighting stance. Whoever this sick pile of garbage was, Dasher was not going to stand for taunting. The thick Spanish accent put Dasher on edge, hastily assuming that whoever this stranger was, he did not have United States citizenship. Though citizenship has no bearing on any human's propensity for kindness or intrinsic contributions to this world, Dasher trusted Americans a hell of a lot more than he trusted anyone even remotely foreign. He didn't care if it was Europe or Mexico. Dasher preferred someone with half the intelligence so long as they were a fundamentalist Christian, devout Republican and looked exactly like him.

Dasher, of course, failed to account for the enormous Latin population that both lived in the United States and offered incredible cultural contributions that helped shift the trajectory of the country. Dasher could not grasp the concept of tacos when things like steak dinners existed, even though tacos oftentimes contained the steak in question. He couldn't conceive anyone living outside of his rudimentary understanding of the human experience, which consisted mostly of prayer, murder, and irrational judgment, in no particular order.

Dasher looked around wildly, trying to determine where the voice had come from. The smell of incense had been replaced by the smell of tobacco, which comforted Dasher because, although still a vice, it wouldn't send whoever was smoking it straight to hell. They would likely only have to exist in purgatory for several centuries before having to beg and plead at the pearly gates to get in. Many good men on his Special Forces team had smoked and that was a hell of a group of men. He looked forward to seeing them all in heaven several years after he had immediately gained entry.

"How do you know my name?" Dasher said, attempting to calm himself down and avoid expending any more energy.

"Dasher, you are a very popular man," said the figure.

Just as he finished the sentenced, Dasher threw several punches where the sound had come from, but only came up with air. The figure was remarkably quick. Dasher continued and threw a spin kick, knocking over what felt like a bookcase, and smashing several bottles. Though the person hadn't been an immediate threat, Dasher knew it was only a matter of time before he turned. They always turned. As Dasher loaded up enough energy for another combination of punches and kicks, he felt a prick in his neck. He recognized it immediately as a rhinoceros tranquilizer. Dasher thought back to the time he took a local youth group to a neglected petting zoo in Gary, Indiana and one of the 7-year-old kids discharged a goat tranquilizer gun into Dasher's neck after a heated exchange about gay marriage. Though he was frustrated, he was proud of a kid for having the balls to pull the trigger. They ended up having a laugh about the whole thing while they fed the goats their deceased brothers and sisters. Dasher collapsed on what felt like a coffee table, glass shattering everywhere.

Meanwhile, the mercenaries lay awake looking at the stars, waiting for a sleep that would never come. Each one dreamt of the hunt that would take place the following day. Each one hoping to unleash a lifetime of insecurities into Duke Dasher. He would pay for what he did, pay for what he stood for. He would pay for the sins of this country. Soon enough, Dasher would be dead.

Unknown Home,
Montana,
United States

Dasher blinked his eyes open. A sensation he had not experienced for several days or weeks. He stared up at the ceiling above; though his vision was blurry, it was there. Like Bartimaeus, Dasher was blind and now he could see. He struggled to sit up; every bone in his body hurt. He immediately disregarded the pain and recalled a phrase he claimed to have invented in his Special Forces team, "Pain is just weakness leaving the body." His team did not have the heart to tell him that it was a poster in virtually every cross-fit gym across the country. Dasher also claimed to invent the phrase, "Don't Tread on Me," which his team also begrudgingly congratulated him on. Dasher's imaginary successes were a crucial part of his personality because he was incapable of original thought. The delusional claims helped provide the flimsy straw padding that kept Dasher propped up on a daily basis. To Dasher's surprise, someone had already created flags and merchandise with the phrases on them, which caused him to become quite paranoid about "the internet" stealing his ideas. He had several lengthy discussions with trademark lawyers who were confused at best.

The first phrase was also not applicable here, as it was not a cross-fit gym and was instead referencing third-degree burns across Dasher's entire body and likely multiple injuries to internal organs. He gritted his teeth and sat up anyway. He didn't have time to be hurt.

"You need your rest Dasher," said the voice. That familiar Spanish accent came from somewhere near the crackling fireplace.

"You were in bad shape Dasher. You know, you really should take better care of yourself, friend," continued the voice.

Dasher immediately remembered the tranquilizer dart penetrating his neck and the subsequent fall into the coffee table, which likely only elevated his current state.

"If you're going to kill me, just get it over with," Dasher said defeated. "I'm too tired for any of your bullshit."

"I'm here to help you," said the man, which somehow was not evident to Dasher even after his vision had been repaired along with the rest of his wounds dressed.

"My name is Mikel Serone. I'm the village healer around these parts," said Serone.

"No offense, but you don't exactly look like you graduated from Johns Hopkins," said Dasher, whose rigid idealized version of a doctor also did not include women.

Serone looked downright whimsical in a flowing poncho with graying long hair. He wore no shoes and his brown eyes looked like they had bared witness to the creation of earth 6,000 years ago. His face was concurrently young and old, covered in wrinkles, but each wrinkle held a pocket of skin with untold wisdom. That is what anyone observing Mikel Serone would have seen, but Dasher saw what he considered a confused elderly man who had treated him against his will and who was not an accredited doctor. He, in fact, did not look Christian in the slightest. Yet somehow, he had taken Dasher into his home and helped him when no one else would, which was the definition of a Christian. Dasher's brain scrambled to make sense of the conflicting signals being sent.

"I am a healer Dasher. Notice how you have your vision back. I made a special blend of herbs that counteracted the poison plaguing you. I applied a rare mud to your burns to

95

help them heal faster," Serone continued, chuckling warmly at Dasher's confusion.

"There's something you need to see Dasher," Serone said, leaving Dasher to ponder the effects of alternative medicine. Serone turned on the worn television set to the whining banter of two CNN stooges.

We are now receiving reports that ex-Special Forces commander Duke Dasher is responsible for the carnage across the country. He was last seen leaving the White House in a Blackhawk helicopter and has since disappeared. We believe he has activated cells across the country and is trying to topple the United States government in an effort to install a communist regime. Dasher is an ex-military officer and is considered armed and extremely dangerous. Police and citizens with concealed carry arms are advised to shoot to kill.

Dasher looked on completely baffled. This wasn't the first time he had been framed for trying to topple the United States government, nor would it be the last, but it was still shocking nonetheless. Dasher absolutely despised the concept of communism, or any political change for that matter, as it applied to the United States. If the founding fathers wanted communism, they would have damn well said so. The government was perfect in Dasher's eyes, so long as Republican President Alphonso Knudson was the commander-in-chief. Had it been President Obama in office, he would have gladly accepted the rumors and perhaps even made a run at carrying out a military coup.

"Why haven't you turned me in yet?" Dasher said with his arms crossed, staring at Serone.

"Because you can't believe everything you hear," Serone replied, taking a sip from his tea.

What was Serone getting at? How could he trust a complete stranger? Dasher didn't believe in the news either, especially CNN, but this hippie seemed like just the type of coward to turn in a soldier in need. He looked like the type of draft dodger Dasher would typically despise. The kind of woke asshole who would weep after reading a tweet about the injustice of continental breakfast from someone who looked like Alexandria Ocasio Cortez. The type of maudlin cuck who would call his wife his best friend. Dasher shuddered at the thought of being friends with his wife. He considered Stacy his subordinate, or if not subordinate, they were at least incestuous soldiers of church and morality. Nonetheless, unlike the lunatic celebrity pastor who was attempting to murder his child, this peaceful, open minded old man had helped him. Dasher grew frustrated with the challenging emotional thoughts that were shaking his fundamental belief system to its core.

"Why did you help me? We're nothing alike," Dasher repeated, almost despondent after the report he had just heard on CNN.

"We might be more alike than you think Duke. Although I'm not an abrasive fundamentalist with a body count totaling in the thousands, I also want what's best for this country. People can be different but want the same thing," said Serone calmly. "You can tell a lot from a man's eyes and from his past," continued Serone. "That, and I also witnessed the horrific car accident you were in with those four other unsavory looking strangers. They looked like the type to inflict hell."

"I see what you're saying. Old-timers like us don't change; we can't change, nor should we," Dasher replied knowingly. Maybe Serone was not so bad. Perhaps he understood that once you took a position on something, you refused to retreat, even when evidence showed that viewpoint to be entirely backward. Dasher was beginning to understand this mysterious shaman more and more, or so he thought.

Serone looked on for several seconds, wondering if Dasher had actually heard anything he said. The man who held an untold number of Purple Hearts and Congressional Medals of Honor seemed to struggle mightily with basic emotions and conversation. Nonetheless, Serone needed to help this man; inexplicably, he was the last, albeit bleak, hope this country deserved.

"Coffee?" asked Serone.

"Extra black," Dasher replied, grinning and already feeling more like himself.

Those special herbs and potions had accelerated Dasher's recovery time by tenfold. Usually, when injured, Dasher would simply take pre-workout supplements and pray the pain away. These herbs actually seemed to be healing him. Dasher and Serone discussed the methods for healing Serone had employed in detail. Dasher sat looking confused and fascinated. For the first time in a long time, he didn't have anything to say. No religious interjections, no moral high ground, just two men of opposite constitutions discussing alternative medicine in a remote cabin in Montana. Dasher was utterly captivated by the use of mud as a skin protectant and the use of plants as a method for detecting intruders. Serone also told Dasher about meditation and spirituality, being in tune with nature and other basic wellness principles. After the two discussed the varying practices in length and had a healthy debate on medium vs. medium-rare steak, Dasher paused for several seconds.

"Have you been baptized, Serone?" Dasher said quizzically.

"Oh...I don't..." started Serone.

"I ask because those men are coming to kill us and despite our differences, I would hate to see a fine man such as yourself condemned to eternal damnation," continued Dasher. "I'm not saying I expect to die, but the Lord works in mysterious ways my friend; and though I'm not expecting it, you better believe I'm ready for it."

Serone sat in the brutally uncomfortable silence like someone suffering through the stench of an asparagus piss by a coworker at an office urinal. He waited for Dasher to excuse himself or say something to diffuse the horrible awkwardness, but Dasher's face remained unchanged, as apathetic as a member of the Blue Man Group on their fourteenth identical show of the week.

99

"Maybe we can discuss this after we figure out how to not die today," Serone said, offering Dasher the hope he sought of converting another person to Christianity.

"I like the way you think Serone; send them to hell before they can send us to heaven," Dasher said with that familiar, deranged grin. Again, Serone's head tilted quizzically. It wasn't necessarily what he meant, but he reckoned it was close enough. The two began preparations on the house to even the playing field. The mercenaries would have no idea what hit them when these two unlikely comrades put their heads together. When the stalking henchman came, Dasher and Serone would be ready.

8 The Hunters Become the Hunted

Somewhere in the woods,
Montana,
United States

Addison Beach, Titus Rains, Hisan and Joel Oscreen woke
the next morning after a restless slumber - the type of
sleep that follows a weekend binger when your chest feels
empty and your lungs feel like they are made of the turned
cantaloupe from an Edible Arrangements forgotten at the
doorstep of a lover lost. Though they didn't talk, each of
them secretly hoped they would be the first to encounter
Dasher. The riches and glory that would come once Popov
found out about the heroics would be untold. Each one
was making calculations for where they would fall in this
new regime and the man who captured or killed Duke
Dasher would have a potential claim at being the new
benevolent leader's right-hand man.

"I'm sure, like me, you guys didn't sleep much. Joel, your
mouth breathing and sleep apnea was very disturbing,"
said Hisan, breaking the awkward silence that sets in
between colleagues in the morning.

"Yes, I don't have my mask, which helps me breathe, and
there are no sockets or electricity out here, so it would
have been useless anyway," replied Oscreen sorrowfully.

"Beach, Rains, will you cool it sharpening those blades?
We have guns and all the ammo we need. What would you
need a machete for?" Hisan said to the two psychopaths
sitting on a log sharpening two substantial blades.

Neither replied. Beach simply took his blade and licked it from bottom to top. The rest wondered what would happen if they didn't find Dasher. Would the maniac known as Addison Beach turn on them? Had the poison that Popov infused in his body corrupted his brain? All extremely reasonable questions, as having your blood and skin replaced with poison would likely pervert the mind in some way. Hisan hoped he wasn't around when Beach truly started to lose it. The man seemed to grow more unglued by the minute.

"Rains, you take the northern quadrant, Beach you're south, Oscreen you're west, I'll head east," continued Hisan, pointing to the various parts in the forest with his silenced 9MM.

There was some protest that followed. Everyone was suspicions that Hisan already scouted the forest and knew Dasher was lurking somewhere in the east quadrant, but the men reluctantly agreed. Paranoia had fully set in the group - each man seemed to be a likely candidate for betrayal, but for now, their mission was to find and capture or kill Duke Dasher.

The men split and Hisan walked stoically towards his quadrant while the others ran like hounds on all fours in their respective directions. Each one was hopeful Dasher would be nothing more than a helpless, burned insect by the time they found him, imagining Dasher's corpse as a burned up mangled mess that Willy Wonka would stuff into a barely edible chocolate bar. He was their golden ticket to fame and fortune in the new communist empire.

Titus Rains began frantically searching the woods, his camouflage intact. This was the advantage Rains held over any adversary. He could see them, but they couldn't see him. After years of intense interrogation and reprogramming, Rains was a shell of his former self - a war tool crafted by the sick, gnarled hooves of Popov, who had personally put Rains through the painful surgery to make him appear invisible. Popov told Rains he would not understand it now, but he needed to be used as a biblical metaphor at some point in the future to capture a man named Duke Dasher. Even in Rains' diminished mental capacity, the idea seemed delusional at best but after several more hours of torture, Rains agreed to become the darkness.

Popov selected a very special doctor to perform the surgery - celebrity psychologist, Dr. Bill. Dr. Bill existed in the same realm of peculiarity as Joel Oscreen. They both appeared to be physically deteriorating before your very eyes. Unmistakably human in some ways and in other ways, vacant and fiendish. A cheap imitation of another balding celebrity doctor with a thick southern accent and a non-existent license in psychology. Both of his eyes once slipped from his sockets and into his lap on live television, a white substance with the same consistency as cottage cheese pouring from each eyehole. He coolly placed them back in while the crowd stood and applauded. Some wept; some maintained that it was the second coming of Christ. No one seemed to know or care why two identical-looking unlicensed doctors were distributing ill-informed advice on TV, but they all limply watched the show daily with nothing better to do.

Even though Dr. Bill maintained he did not have a medical degree, Popov had been confident he was the perfect man for the job. The other celebrity doctor would have been far too challenging to kidnap. Popov had sent an undercover operative claiming to be Dr. Bill's bastard child on *The Dr. Bill Show*. Dr. Bill had immediate suspicions because he knew he had not fathered any mystery children and the man claiming to be his son was his age if not older, which made the circumstances almost impossible. After realizing the reasonable suspicions by Dr. Bill, the henchman had forcibly kidnapped him instead, making the entire backstory of being his bastard child completely pointless. It was precisely what Popov had envisioned. The type of seamlessly executed stealth missions the Russians were known for. Dr. Bill had injected Swarovski crystals with a homemade mixture of Elmer's-like glue into the skin of Titus Rains. The reflective properties on a crystal as rare and unblemished as a Swarovski created an illusion in which the person almost disappeared.

Dr. Bill objected to the procedure from both a medical and a basic rudimentary logic perspective. Elmer's glue did not seem to be the most quality adhesive for what they were attempting to accomplish and Swarovski crystals were generally reserved for uneducated losers going into debt for a marriage that would inevitably fail. However, after several tantrums thrown by Popov, Dr. Bill went ahead with the procedure, which took several hours. Dr. Bill was then driven to rural Ohio and released into a retention pond outside of a Costco. Popov looked at Titus Rains as he lay on the table. He saw the effects of the procedure set in almost immediately.

Rains began disappearing before his eyes. Popov took a hefty pull from the handle of vodka he was drinking and rubbed his eyes as though they were playing tricks on him. The procedure had actually worked and what lay before him was someone who would be an integral tool in killing Duke Dasher and toppling the United States government.

Rains continued to walk through the woods, careful not to disturb any leaves or brush, remaining completely and utterly invisibly. Even if Dasher was injured, he could still be dangerous, and there was nothing more dangerous than a wounded, ex-Special Forces, fundamentalist Christian hell-bent on revenge. Rains wandered throughout the forest until, in the distance, he noticed an anomaly. Blood on the ground. He bent down and smelled the blood, then tasted it. It was undoubtedly human. He looked down at the brush and there appeared to be a steady skid mark all in one direction. Either Dasher had crawled in the direction of the blood flow or a raccoon was throwing up blood after eating the tin of Bush's baked beans that Rains had bizarrely laced with glass shards and left out as a trap the night before. Rains despised raccoons. Either scenario was a possibility, but he hoped for the former. He slowly followed the path of unnerving blood-colored ivy.

Unknown Home,
Montana,
United States

Dasher and Serone sat around the small, wooden kitchen table drinking their coffee after a long night of work.

They spent the entire night preparing for what could be their last day on earth. Dasher also made several more desperate attempts to convert Serone to Christianity and, at one point, created a S.W.O.T. analysis board detailing the path to a successful conversion. There was noticeably nothing in the threats or weaknesses portion of the board. Though Serone had tried to focus primarily on the task of saving their lives, Dasher pressed on with several lectures dripping in fire and brimstone propaganda. Serone attempted time and again to maintain a semblance of politeness, but Dasher was becoming downright insufferable. One could only endure being bludgeoned with stale points of view and a barrage of one-upping before they finally broke. Serone somewhat regretted ever letting Dasher into his house. If he had dragged him back out into the woods, would he be in his current situation? Serone knew the men that hunted them were dangerous and he would have to deal with them eventually. He was better off with Dasher than without him.

The two finished off their cups of coffee and for the first time in about eight hours, there was silence. The two mutually understood that whatever shit storm was blowing their way was about to hit. They both went to the positions they agreed upon and waited - waited for whatever was coming their way.

Dasher sat in a tree while Serone crouched under an enormous wooden box they had constructed. A tree branch held up the box with a string tied to it, which Dasher held between his fingers. When any enemy arrived to attack the helpless Serone, Dasher would pull the string

107

that would dislodge the stick and trap the intruder inside the box. Serone pleaded for a different capture tactic, as this particular method left him initially vulnerable and also stranded with whomever the intruder was inside the box. Dasher was known for his persistence though and Serone had trouble arguing with the decades of military experience Dasher had accrued. Maybe he knew something Serone did not. Either that or he was merely sacrificing Serone's life to save his own. All of this passed through Serone's head as he sat inside a giant box fully nude. Dasher insisted this was the most essential part of the entire plan - Serone must be fully nude. Dasher radioed down to Serone.

"Serone, can you hear me?" Dasher asked through the static of the walkie-talkie.

"I can hear you. Dasher, are you sure this is going to work?" Serone asked nervously.

"Believe me Serone, you put the bait out, an animal is going to take it. They can't help themselves because, unfortunately, they don't interpret remorse and sinning the same way we do," Dasher said longingly.
He wished every creature experienced the same agonizing shame humans did.

Serone sat in silence for several seconds, contemplating dying in this giant box by the hands of a total lunatic. The quiet was disrupted when he saw a slight rustle in the bushes ahead. The bush had definitely moved, but there was nothing there. How could this be? Maybe it was the wind. Maybe it was Serone's mind playing tricks on him. Then it happened again. This time it was closer.

"Dasher, do you see anything up there?" whispered Serone. No response from Dasher.

"Dasher, do you read me?" Serone whispered again, this time more frantically.

Still no response from Dasher. He had gone completely dark. Just as Serone decided to bolt from the giant box trap Dasher had constructed, something appeared in front of him. It was screaming at the top of its lungs and was covered in some sort of sticky substance. A fan was then initiated in front of a patch of dandelions, which stuck to the sticky mess in front of him, revealing the outline shape of a man. Dasher jumped down from the trees chuckling.

"You really taught me something Serone," Dasher said playfully.

Serone stood in complete shock, confused as to what was going on. The man was now doubled over on the ground. His face and skin appeared to be melting and dripping through the weeds on the forest floor. Smoke was emanating from the bursting skin bubbles.

"You taught me about using nature to do your bidding, Serone. I used your same healing technique to maim this mercenary. The tree sap covering his skin counteracted his invisibility," Dasher continued, patting Serone on the shoulder.

"Dasher, I'm not sure you…" started Serone.

"Believe me, Serone. I understood exactly what you meant when we were talking about spirituality and meditation, so I took your healing techniques and applied them to warfare. Now this man's skin is melting off of his body and being picked apart by those insects!" interrupted Dasher.

The two could barely hear each other talk over the deafening screams of the man lying on the ground. It was a truly disgusting sight, even for Dasher, who had seen a lot in his lifetime. He looked on at the pathetic loser writhing around and gave it a quick kick to the stomach in an attempt to shut him up. Serone could not take his eyes off the man, how could someone be in this much pain and more importantly, why was he melting?

"I knew something was up when I was taken by surprise back at my house. Someone had snuck in on me, so I knew that some type of camouflage was at play," Dasher explained, taking advantage of the brief break in screaming. "I then microwaved around 20 gallons of tree sap and set up a tripwire that would dump the smoldering hot sap on whoever walked under it. The dandelions served merely as humiliation, which is an important part when dealing with any enemy," Dasher continued as he flicked the tripwire he had created.

Serone wished Dasher had explained some of the plans to him before making him crawl under that enormous box nude, especially given that he walked the path that Dasher

110

had chosen to suspend the box of liquid hot tree sap
above, but he was relieved to be alive. Dasher bent down
to the body that seized uncontrollably before him.

"Why are you trying to kill me!" Dasher
demanded, booting the corpse in the head and knocking it
clean off its body. The head rolled twenty feet into the
distance. Serone could not believe his eyes; he instantly
puked, but gave Dasher a bashful thumbs up when Dasher
glanced back at him. The burning sap had caused severe
deterioration of skin and bone, making the head fly off the
neck like candles on a birthday cake.

"Dead men tell no tales. Go fetch that head if you will,"
Dasher said to Serone. Serone wandered begrudgingly into
the woods to retrieve the head. He had no idea what
Dasher had planned, but given what had already occurred,
he assumed it to be some type of very particular biblical-
themed revenge.

South Quadrant,
Forest,
Montana

Addison Beach heard the scream instantly. His ears perked
up, as did something else. The sick bastard had always
been aroused by the prospect of slaughter. If he wasn't
mistaken, it was the scream of his colleague Titus Rains.
Most men would have been disappointed that an ally was
maimed beyond comprehension, or what sounded like it
anyway, but this just meant one less person to steal his

glory when he presented Dasher's corpse to Popov.

His relationship had been rather precarious with Popov given the fact that the man had filled his body with poison and routinely beat the living shit out of him for all the years he was stuck in that cage. However, his new powers were unlike anything he could have imagined. When Popov said he would be the most elite killer this world has ever seen, Beach had jumped at the opportunity. He was a man who had plateaued in many ways; his life had grown boring after retiring from the Green Berets. Maybe it was the poison that was killing thousands of brain cells every minute, but Beach felt fortunate to have been kidnapped by Popov. He never could have achieved this level of power without the help from a sadistic lunatic willing to push the boundaries of medicine in order to create the perfect killing machine. The drawback was, of course, being completely and utterly alone at all times and virtually every piece of food he ate tasted like dehydrated dog shit. He also had a severe case of erectile dysfunction, routine anal fissures, moderate to severe plaque psoriasis, and regularly battled with mesothelioma for which he was seeking a settlement. Outside of those very extreme and sad ailments that made daily existence insufferable at best, his life was nearly perfect.

The poison had also put him in a perpetual state of hallucination in which he was frequently unable to determine reality versus fantasy. This, in some ways, made him an even more unstoppable soldier, as he was utterly fearless and deranged, only obsessed with poisoning as many people as possible. Popov had sent him on countless missions prior to this one, where he had repeatedly proved his willingness to the cause.

His final mission had been a visit to his parent's house. Beach recognized the house as Popov pulled up in his leased, cherry red, Chrysler Sebring convertible.

"I can tell you recognize this place," Popov had said, slurring horribly. His voice sent a shiver up Beach's spine, not because he recognized the house, but because he had just driven with a man who was clearly blackout drunk.

"This is my parent's house. Say, do you think I could drive home?" Beach had responded, still fearing for his life with Popov behind the wheel. Popov belched and blew into Beach's face it smelled oddly like the tapioca pudding served at a nursing home.

"You know what you have to do to prove yourself to the cause. Your parents are the last remaining thing from your past, and they must be destroyed for you to reach your perfect form, my child," Popov said, throwing in an enormous lip of chewing tobacco, swallowing a substantial amount and immediately spitting up on Beach's jeans.

Beach had listened carefully; at this point in his life, the poison hadn't consumed his brain the way it had presently. He understood that to achieve his perfect form, he had to burn down virtually everything from his past. He unbuckled his seat belt and made the slow walk to his house. He contemplated what being a part of Popov's elite team of assassins truly meant.

He opened the door and called in. "Mum? Dad?" No response. He called again. He walked up the old familiar stairs perhaps for the last time.

"Addison, what in God's name is going on down there?" his dad asked angrily. "Who is that drunk in that piece of shit convertible that knocked over all of our damn trash cans!?"

"That drunk is my new father," Addison said under his breath.

"New father or not, you better tell him to pick up those trash cans or I swear I'm lodging a formal complaint with the condo association a get your ass evicted, so help me, God!" replied Beach's dad.

Addison had gone back downstairs silently. He poured three glasses of wine and stuck his poisoned finger in the glistening Sutter Home, then brought them back upstairs.

"A toast," Addison suggested.

"It's four in the damn morning Addison. You really think I want a glass of three- week old Sutter Home? Are you nuts?" his dad replied.

The romance of the murder deflated like a convenient store balloon. Addison had given up on the pageantry of death by convenient store wine and merely grabbed the shoulders of his poor mum and dad. They collapsed instantly, overcome by poison, and a new Addison Beach was born.

In the south quadrant of a forest in rural Montana, Beach shook his head furiously, momentarily casting the memory out of his mind. He sprinted in the direction of his colleague's screams, eager to murder Dasher much like he had killed his parents and prove to Popov that he was the most elite killer in the world.

9 Finding Duke Dasher

Rockford,
Illinois,
United States

Patrick Kibby had palmed the security guard on duty twenty dollars to tell him the coordinates of where the Blackhawk helicopter had crash-landed. The guard had been suspicious of someone whose sloping shoulders, beady eyes and quivering lips made him look perpetually on the verge of breaking down in tears, but ultimately knew the twenty dollars would get him and his wife and kids drunk one more night. Kibby later found himself in rural Illinois. He stopped at a California Pizza Kitchen for a quick bite of Chicago style pizza, as one does in rural Illinois, and then hurried to the coordinates. Wherever this helicopter had landed bore great significance in finding the truth behind the spree of neck snappings happening across the country. What could possibly be at the end of these coordinates? A Plato's Closet? Would it be a mass grave constructed by Dasher for all of his victims? Was this entire predicament as simple as a singular maniac going off the rails like the President had detailed, or was the threat something larger?

Kibby pulled into a non-descript cul-de-sac. The air smelled of potpourri and quitting. The well-manicured lawns served as red carpets for the residents who had abandoned their dreams in favor of insufferable suburban living. "They wouldn't trade their life for anything in the world," Kibby had heard and seen from friends who never left - friends who were trying to devour enough Xanax and produce enough shitty art at wine-and-paints to

117

convince their uninterested social media following they were happy. The yellowing beige walls of each house matched the dull complexion of the people inside. Kibby continued on in disbelief. Up ahead, he spotted the Blackhawk helicopter crashed in front of a ranch-style home with an unreasonably large and budget-friendly looking Don't Tread On Me flag flying out front. Kibby wondered again about the President's accusations of Duke Dasher. He pondered if somewhere this benign seeming could really be the catalyst for a nationwide terror crisis.

He pulled wearily into the driveway. Even from the vantage point of his shareable electric scooter, the door to the house appeared completely open. Kibby reached into his back pocket, hoping to God that he had packed his pocket knife, but instead found only a handful of extremely full tissues. It would not have mattered anyway if Dasher were, in fact, at the house. Kibby's skull would be crushed instantly.

He approached the front door, his All Bird sneakers making him appear like even more of a weakling loser than he was. He had fallen for the relentless Facebook ads almost immediately and would talk endlessly to friends about their superior comfort and styling. All the while, he merely appeared to be some blubbering spokesperson for a shoe that screamed gullibility and willingness to be targeted by lifeless marketing techniques.

"Hello?" Kibby yelled in the house, breaching into the foyer while experiencing another breach in the seat of his pants.

"Get the fuck out!" someone yelled from the kitchen. "Girl Scout cookies are more dangerous than vaccinating your children, so get the fuck out!" the voice screamed again.

"I just need to ask you about a certain Duke Dasher. Do you know him?" Kibby asked cautiously. There was a pause for several seconds; Kibby took this as a good sign, hoping the person would be willing to talk.
Instead, he felt his skull caving under a sock full of quarters. The last thing he remembered was watching the blood pool under his head onto a wood floor. When he woke up, he was tied firmly to what appeared to be a life-sized crucifix in a completely white room.

"You awake? When Duke bought this life-sized cross from Sky Mall using the last bit of my inheritance, I thought he had lost his marbles, but this thing is paying dividends now," said the woman standing in front of him. Kibby blinked several times. He knew he was severely concussed, but he had to find out what was going on. Goddamn Sky Mall, thought Kibby, rattling his hands and feet, which were securely tied to the enormous wooden structure.

"Look, I think we're on the same side here. I think the President is lying," blurted out Kibby, realizing he was also now missing several teeth. He wondered how that had happened, given it seemed like the person had hit him from behind.

"I see you licking your teeth. I pulled a few of them when you weren't answering me during our first interrogation. I guess you were still asleep," said the person holding up a Ziploc bag full of teeth.

"Are you Stacy Dasher?" said Kibby, now with a severe lisp.

"All my life," replied Stacy Dasher.

Stacy Dasher was a legend in the philanthropic world. Kibby wondered how the woman in front of him could be the same person. She seemed erratic and paranoid. The news of Dasher's exploits delivered by the President must have caused a complete mental breakdown.

"Stacy, I think your husband is being framed. Something about the President...I can't tell what, but I think Dasher is being set up," continued Kibby. "I need your help in finding evidence to clear his name."

Stacy took a hero line of blue powder from the edge of a military knife directly into her nose. Her head jerked back and when it leveled, her nose hemorrhaged blood all over Kibby's whimpering face; his discomfort didn't seem to concern her.

"That's the first smart thing you've said all day," Stacy said, spitting on Kibby's coveted All Bird sneakers.

"I already told the president everything. Joel Oscreen came here with three men and tried to murder us before kidnapping Duke and taking him away in a Honda Civic. God, Duke always hated driving foreign. He must have been madder than a wet hen," continued Stacy, in a Southern accent of sorts.

"Why didn't the President listen? This all seems to hold up based on what I've researched," asked Kibby.

"He said Joel Oscreen has never done anything wrong that he's ever seen, so, therefore, Joel would never have taken Duke. He also expressed mistrust because I am regrettably, a woman," replied Stacy.

The logic seemed sound enough for someone running the most powerful country in the world. Kibby shook his head in dismay. All of this time, Duke had a potential alibi. Could he really trust Stacy Dasher, who was now in the corner changing her own adult diaper? He did not have a choice. After several hours of rabid debate and negotiation to get himself untied, a deal was finally struck. He told Stacy that if she released him, he would order a Harry & David gift basket to the house and put her hair in cornrows with seashells at the tips as they do at fancy Mexican all-inclusive resorts. The improbable combination was strange enough to appease someone as unglued as Stacy Dasher. Once untied, Kibby explained his method for winning Duke Dasher's public approval back.

"First things first. I publish the article *Top 10 times Duke Dasher Beheaded a Terrorist while Singing an Acapella National*

Anthem with a Nude Pentatonix Cover Band. If it goes viral like I think, it'll immediately sway the fickle country back into Duke's corner," Kibby said excitedly, knowing that the headline alone would persuade the swarms of locusts barely able to wipe their own asses back into Dasher's corner.

The country existed almost exclusively on lists, rankings, and short form videos. Always favoring the most recent anal bead dripping with reheated content being popped into their gaping assholes. Week-old news passed through their system like a can of room temperature creamed corn. Kibby published the article and hoped the flies would dutifully swarm the shit sandwich served on crumbling Wonder Bread.

"Next thing, is there anything we could use to locate Dasher like a cell phone or pager? Did you maybe hear the men say where they were taking him?" Kibby asked.

"A condom filled to the brim with blood," Stacy replied knowingly, even though the response elicited a disturbed look from Kibby.

"Excuse me?" said Kibby. "A condom full of blood? I thought Dasher was strictly opposed to contraceptives."

"His hatred of contraceptives is well documented, but this was bought at a gift shop in the Vatican when we went. The store owner told us it was the blood of Judas. It reeked like gasoline…there was certainly blood in it too, but mostly gasoline. I knew it wasn't an actual relic, but

Duke seemed so excited…" Stacy replied, experiencing what appeared to be either a moment of clarity or severe and uncontrollable gas. A moment later, it was confirmed to be the latter.

"Sorry Stacy, but I'm having trouble following. It seems like Dasher may or may not have purchased a condom that a complete stranger filled with gasoline and possibly their own blood. I don't understand how this is relevant in finding Duke," said Kibby. He glanced down and saw the likes and shares growing on the article he had published.

"There was a car accident outside of Montana last week; witnesses said the car spontaneously burst into flames. None of the people in the car were found, and the car was not found either. It came through on our police scanner," replied Stacy, already grabbing a soiled jean jacket from Burlington Coats.

Kibby followed closely behind. Stacy Dasher may have been nuts, but this was the only lead he had, so he followed purposefully. She had also threatened to "cut his junk off" if he didn't come along, so the rescue mission was concurrently a hostage situation also. Kibby was all right with it, so long as he got the truth and his scrotum remained intact.

10 Old Testament, Bloodlust and a Hairy Denver Omelette

Unknown Home,
Montana,
United States

Serone's stomach was still turning from the appalling image of Dasher melting a man to death and then booting his head twenty feet into a thorn bush. The nickname of "God Hand" was certainly being displayed in its full might. Dasher wielded power with all the carelessness of a drunk lighting the wrong end of a cigarette. Serone was still grateful to be alive, but he hoped the next method of survival wouldn't shatter him emotionally like the first one did.

"Serone, you're looking a little yellow over there. You never saw a man's head turn into scrambled eggs huh?" chuckled Dasher, as he knelt down working very hard on something. "Looked like a Denver omelet at Denny's, didn't it? Clumps of hair and all!" Dasher continued.

He grunted one last time and stood up to reveal a stick sagging over with the decapitated head hanging from it like an enormous ornament on Charlie Brown's Christmas tree. Dasher had formed the face into an infuriatingly smug smile.

"Dasher, what the hell have you done!?" screamed Serone.

"This time, you don't have to be the bait," Dasher said, giving Serone a slight nudge. He pressed a small button in his hand and the sickening remains of the head lit up. "Let there be light," continued Dasher. He then went on a twelve-minute rant about how the destroyed head was technically similar to when God granted the universe he created with light. Serone nodded, unable to take his eyes off the dripping sculpture in front of him.

"I don't celebrate Halloween because it's a holiday for the devil, but maybe I should start!" Dasher laughed as he examined his handy work on the head. "I'm just kidding with you Serone. I would kill myself before celebrating that heathen holiday," Dasher continued in a profoundly stern tone.

Serone's head instinctively nodded as it had been doing since he met Dasher. Absolutely nothing could be said about the objectively awful scene before them.

Dasher detailed the plan in which they would use the light within the head to signal SOS to the comrades they had not slaughtered yet. When Serone asked about the feasibility of someone ramming a flashlight down his or her throat and then using it to signal for help instead of a walkie-talkie, Dasher stared at him as if he was crazy before returning to the final part of the plan. Serone was just happy to be a part of the program this time instead of sitting completely nude in a crudely fashioned box. Dusk approached and Dasher gloated that this was already a successful first step in his plan. Then, they heard someone rustling in the forest.

"Get your popcorn ready Serone. It's go time," said Dasher. Serone was relieved he didn't have to endure any more conversations with Dasher for the moment.

The shrouded figure approached the head carefully, examining it from several angles. Dasher maneuvered the strings in his hand to make it appear as though the mouth was talking.

"Peace be with you," said the face, as Dasher threw his voice in that direction. The head tilted inquisitively as though expecting a response from the figure who gave none.

"Accept this Eucharist and experience salvation," continued the face, but as Dasher yanked the string, the bottom jaw fell limply onto the ground with a dull thud.

The stranger gazed down to a sawn off-hand, missing several fingers and holding a circular piece of cardboard with a cross crudely sketched in permanent marker in the center. Serone stood on, wondering why the absurd interaction had gone on for as long as it did.

A fully-grown man stared at a talking, decapitated head for close to a minute and a half and had just consumed a piece of bread from a bloody stump. Maybe everyone who inhabited this world was equally as sick these two men. Dasher was always the first to explain biblical parallels with the actions he took, but was this what God really wanted? According to Dasher, there was no doubt in his mind. This was the path of the righteous and would fast track Dasher to a spot in heaven. Dasher whipped a knife going a hundred miles an hour at the being's head, but it dodged it seamlessly. Dasher was shocked by its reaction time. It's yellow eyes now focused directly on Dasher and Serone.

"Alright, so you caught us. Now what?" Dasher said to the being.

"Addison Beach. Pleased to make your acquaintance Dasher," Beach said with a childlike bewilderment.

"Life isn't meant to be pleasurable, Beach. Didn't your dad teach you anything?" Dasher snapped coldly. For a brief moment, Beach seemed to take pity on the brute before him.

"Looks like you got your vision back, Dasher," said Beach, his tone both impressed and enraged.

There was a sulfurous smell in the air, as though someone had hardboiled an egg immediately after cooking a tuna melt in a shared office microwave. The same scent that Dasher smelled right before he was blinded. His mind flashed back to what Joel Oscreen said about killing his first-born child and he immediately made the extremely loose connection between the Egyptian plagues and the men trying to kill him. Someone was definitely trying to turn his religion against him and make him mistrust his God through the hands of these mercenaries. Little did they know, Dasher had been blindly following his faith for years with virtually no concern about its archaic approach to the modern world. Three men who had been constructed as representations of the Egyptian plagues in an attempt to kill Dasher served as a mere, loving reminder that he must persevere and never, under any circumstance, change his rigid way of thinking.

"If you haven't guessed already Dasher, I represent pestilence," said Beach, breaking the incredibly awkward silence that had persisted over the last three minutes, during which, it appeared Dasher was deep in thought wrestling with his own spirituality.

"I could have guessed that, Beach. You look like Samson after that whore shaved his head and he got his eyes gouged by the Philistines," said Dasher. The poor attempt at extremely specific biblical humor wilted immediately upon leaving his mouth. Serone offered a sympathetic laugh, which only served to accentuate the pathetic joke.

"Anyways, I will be bringing both of your corpses to Popov soon enough. One touch from my poisonous fingertips and you will wish you had been shot," replied Beach, throwing the gun he had been pointing at them into the weeds.

Dasher was not going to have the luxury of dying by gun; he was going to be forcibly poisoned by this apex predator. Beach approached slowly, the smell of sulfur reaching a frenzy. Dasher pedaled backward in unison with Beach's forward momentum.

"Now, Serone!" yelled Dasher. Serone began painstakingly dragging out a baby pool filled with the mud he had used to cure Dasher's burns.

He dragged the pool for what seemed like an eternity into the clearing where the two men stood. Mud sloshed over the sides of the pool and onto the ground below. His back

129

appeared to give out several times during the endeavor, but Dasher had been explicit in his planning. Dasher slowly stripped naked, never breaking eye contact with Beach. He entered the pool calmly, submerging himself entirely and rising out of the pool with only the whites of his eyes showing, still gazing deeply at Beach. Beach stood, completely stunned at what he was seeing. Serone sprinted back inside the house and retrieved a hairdryer with a lengthy extension cord. He furiously dried the mud on Dasher until no wet spots remained. Dasher's mouth finally opened.

"Didn't expect this, did you Beach? I learned a thing or two about Serone while I was recovering from my burns. You think you're gonna beat me? Well, it will have to be without any of that pussy ass poison you've been boasting about," said Dasher, the mud forming a protective layer on his skin.

"Well then quit it with this preachy goddamn homily and let's do this," replied Beach.

"I can live with getting poisoned and going blind; what I can't live with is you taking the Lord's name in vain," said Dasher.

The two men sprinted at each other. Serone was ready for the fight of a lifetime - two warriors trained in multiple martial arts battling to the death. Two trained killers who held the honor of fighting over everything. Combatants who would give everything they had to prove they were the superior soldier. No guns, no knives. This was a matter of who was more of a man. Before they had touched each other, Dasher reached into a bush and grabbed a sawed-off shotgun. He approached Beach and blew one of his legs clean off. Serone's prior assumptions about the confrontation were proven wrong. Serone threw up once more. Dasher walked up to the screaming Addison Beach, who was cursing and crying.

"What have you done, Dasher? I thought we agreed to no weapons!" shouted Beach, thrashing on the ground and spraying blood on anything within a three-foot radius.

"I've made three agreements in my life: one to my God, one to my country and one to my wife, in that order," replied a sneering Dasher.

He reached Beach and asked him what he meant by delivering their bodies to Popov. Before Beach could answer, he jammed the shotgun as far as he could down his throat and blew his head clean off, spraying bone fragments and grey brain matter into an enormous sopping wet spider web on the floor of the forest. Serone lay in the fetal position on the ground several feet away. The awesome power of Dasher, combined with the grotesqueness of the slaughter at hand, had simply overwhelmed him.

"Dasher, I'm trying to figure out why we had to fill that baby pool with mud and then spend several minutes awkwardly blow drying you if you just had a shotgun in the bush the entire time," Serone said several minutes after recovering from the scene of the murder.

"Optical illusion Serone, much like Jesus turning water into wine, classic misdirection," replied Dasher.

"You don't think God would willingly encourage people to sin by drinking do you? It was an optical illusion, and thus the most impressive miracle in the Bible in some ways. Serone...you were technically part of a modern-day miracle today," Dasher laughed, his explanation making Serone wonder if he had ever actually read the Bible before.

Serone pondered how turning a man's head into 60/40 ground beef on a forest floor qualified as a miracle, but he supposed Dasher knew the qualifications better than he did.

"An eye for an eye," Dasher continued flippantly, walking back towards Serone. "Gonna have to do a few Hail Mary's for that one," laughed Dasher, referencing the potential penance he would get when he confessed to his most recent body count. Thankfully, several Hail Mary's would wipe his slate completely clean no matter if the kills were justified or not. The thought of unlimited chances at heaven through confession comforted Dasher greatly.

"We just evened the playing field Serone. Now we do the hunting," said Dasher.

Serone had no idea what he possibly meant by them now hunting. After all, wasn't trapping and brutally murdering your subject technically hunting? Serone dreamt of the moment where he would abandon Dasher and immediately seek out therapy and perhaps several strong prescriptions that would make him numb enough to aimlessly wander through life.

11 The United States of Grain Alcohol

White House,
Washington D.C.,
United States

President Knudson paced around his office. If you could call the slow, labored strides he took pacing. It was more of a dismal limp. His lungs burned and an extremely productive cough birthed from his chest. He held onto his desk and hawked a sizeable phlegm-riddled wad of spittle roughly the size of a billiards cue ball. He wondered where the hell Dasher had gone and who the hell had published that Buzzfeed article that was swaying public favor back towards Dasher.

Knudson saw the Buzzfeed article while browsing a recent onslaught of Kim Kardashian butt pictures. It was an infuriating disruption to his daily ritual and his once omnipotent power was now being questioned again. All it took was a top 10 list for the public to start asking questions. One list for them to challenge the slop they had been mindlessly eating while waiting to be slaughtered. He had his intern compile several tweets regarding the earth's flatness, but they had only been moderately successful in turning the public's attention away from what had become known as the "Dasher Dilemma." Protests both in opposition and support of Dasher consumed the country, oftentimes growing as violent as the neck snappings that had sparked the initial unrest. The President's public remarks on Dasher had served as gasoline for the dumpster fire that lurked in the seedy underbelly of the United States.

Irrational accusations had always been successful in the past, but for some reason, it hadn't entirely worked this time. The country was evolving before his very eyes and it terrified him. He shuffled over to the bathtub he had demanded be installed in his office and drew himself a room-temperature bath. He walked to the kitchen and plugged in a toaster, slowly running the cord through his hands, making sure he had enough to reach the tub he was about to climb into. He took a long pull from his bottle of computer duster and mounted the bathtub, preparing for submersion, accepting failure was the only thing left to do. The interns in his office raised their eyebrows at each other, but they had been explicitly instructed to never interfere with any Presidential matters, and this was assuredly a Presidential matter. Just as the President climbed into the tub with the toaster, a phone buzzed on his desk.

The President wrestled against his wet flapping skin to pry himself from the tub that would shortly be his tomb. He didn't recognize the phone on his desk and wasn't sure who had placed it there. After thirty seconds or so of helpless flailing, he managed to turn the bath over completely and erupted onto the floor of his office, spilling the stinking water all over the shag carpeting. He crawled towards the phone, looking to treat himself to one more glimpse of blue light before ending it all, and the presence of the mysterious telephone had stirred something in the empty pit of his stomach. His soft hands and bloated fingers fumbled with the flip phone before finally opening it.

"President Knudson, you seem to be in quite a bit of trouble," said the garbled voice.

"I'm doing just fine, thank you!" said Knudson, looking over the flipped tub, the plugged-in toaster, and the several inches of water being soaked into the moldy carpet. The room looked anything but fine.

"We both know that's not accurate," said the voice.

"Is this Eric? Eric, I already said I'm not donating any more money to your sex-specific athleisure wear company," said Knudson.

His son Eric had been desperately trying to make a line of clothing that finally bridged the gap between athletic wear, leisurewear, and cloths explicitly made for erotic purposes. Knudson had seen the craftsmanship on the pair of crotchless jogger pants and had donated several thousand dollars, but a manufacturing issue in China had delayed the pants from ever being seen stateside. Knudson then wondered what had ever happened to the dry-fit gag ball that his son had also pitched and reminisced on squandered potential.

"This is someone who is very important to you right now Mr. President," continued the distorted voice.

"You explain who the hell you are right now or I hang this phone up. I have very important business to attend to," replied Knudson, carefully selecting a good thumbnail from PornHub on his iPad and redrawing his bath.

"I can make this all go away and make you a god," replied the voice.

"I'm listening," said the President; he was willing to do anything to maintain leverage over the political plunger he was using to pump the country into the shit-filled sewers where it belonged.

The voice was none other than Vladimir Popov, who was drunk out of his mind on Southern Comfort. He thoroughly explained his plot to the President, telling him that their common enemy was Duke Dasher and if he could be eradicated, they could both be men of transcendent power in the newly installed communist regime. President Knudson was very interested. Not only would it get him out of the current predicament he was in, but he would be more unstoppable than ever, virtually untouchable, even by Dasher if he were still alive. Popov had the President right where he wanted him and he knew it. The chaos he created had divided the country and the President was desperate for a lifeline.

The prospect certainly intrigued the president, but Popov's main selling point was the elaborate cloning facilities that had been built and were actively producing clones of notable American celebrities for the past several years.

"We knew your people were stupid, but we didn't realize just how stupid! We've been producing cheap knock-offs of virtually every B-List celebrity in the country and people have lapped out of their dirty diapers like dogs," said Popov in between dry heaving and demanding

McDonald's from his beleaguered assistant. "Currently, these celebrities are responsible for simply creating intolerable content, but little do they know, these celebrity clones are also soldiers of the resistance," continued Popov.

The celebrities had apparently been implanted with a Russian-made chip that, when adjusted, would turn them into ruthless killing machines. Popov explained that he had tested the mechanism with celebrity pastor Joel Oscreen, who was currently hunting down and killing Dasher. The President giggled with excitement as he dipped a three-day-old Papa John's breadstick into a healthy portion of garlic oil and rubbed it around his mouth before finally delighting himself with a bite. Popov listened to the nauseating lip smacking for several seconds before finally interrupting the uncanny ritual. The President imagined Simon Crowell, the host of the show *America's Got Gout*, instilling order in the slums of America with a jetpack and a bazooka. Something like this was the utopia he had always fantasized about. The cheapened celebrities were undeniably attractive and more attainable than their realistic counterparts were. It gave the nation hope and instilled a sense of pride. Having these same celebrities function as ruthless minions to their benevolent overlord would be the new American dream.

"What do I need to do?" asked Knudson.
"In three days, I'll give you direction on where to meet me. You must submit to me and pledge your allegiance to new communist empire," said Popov, hacking uncontrollably into the phone.

Although these could have been the simple ramblings of a delusional drunk, something about the way Popov described the plan made it all seem incredibly legitimate. Vladimir Popov had been the puppet master behind many government coups over the last decade. If this were, in fact, Vladimir Popov, and not one of the clones he described, this new government would be installed successfully within the week. President Alphonso Knudson was about to betray his country in favor of ultimate power, the type of exchange young politicians aspire for their entire lives.

12 Dasher's Heart

Montana Interstate,
United States

Patrick Kibby and Stacy Dasher had been driving for what seemed like forever. Stacy had been insufferable and Kibby questioned why they brought her son Terry on what seemed like a dangerous reconnaissance mission. Stacy had been snorting what Kibby believed to be meth for the entirety of the drive. Kibby was forced to listen to Stacy explain the dangers of glory holes to Terry, along with meticulously pulling the breading off of a twenty-piece chicken McNugget box while explaining that carbohydrates caused Dasher to get Low T. Just as Kibby thought he was going to completely break and give up on saving the country, they pulled close to the location of the car that spontaneously exploded, which Stacy had seen on the news. Kibby checked his phone once more. He was surprised and concerned at how viral his article *Top 10 Times Duke Dasher Beheaded a Terrorist while Singing an Acapella National Anthem with a Nude Pentatonix Cover Band* had gone. The intention was not to split the country down the middle, ruin families, and sow distrust in the government, but the article had to be published. All he ever wanted was the truth.

Kibby pulled over to the road, dutifully putting on his hazard signal. Stacy Dasher stumbled out of the car and rinsed her mouth out with a Mountain Dew Code Red. She offered the abused can to Kibby for a similar freshener, but Kibby politely declined. Terry Dasher gnawed on a Yankee Candle in the back seat and stared indifferently out the window. Something had absolutely happened here. There was a visible piece of concrete missing from the shoulder of the road along with an enormous crater where the car had landed, skidded, and finally stopped. Kibby wondered how anyone had missed this, but noticed that the crash site was directly across from an iconic American roadside wonder. The world's largest human fleshlight stood erect with patriotic glory, casting an enormous lecherous shadow on the accident site. A sex toy this large could distract even the most astute police officer or pedestrian. Tempting passersby to take an Instagram to commemorate what would be considered a formative moment in their pathetic lives.

Stacy and Kibby approached the crash site and immediately noticed an extremely apparent trail of blood from the crash site into the forest. Despite Kibby's objections, Stacy maintained that Terry would be fine sitting in the car - she had "left a window cracked."

"That's Duke's blood," Stacy commented, looking at the ominous path into the forest. Kibby didn't bother asking how she could so confidently identify Dasher's blood, but something about her tone made her seem more sure than she had ever been in her life.

"Should we follow it?" Kibby asked nervously. The gravity of the situation suddenly set in.

"Duke wouldn't leave a trail of blood unless he wanted someone to follow it," continued Stacy. Kibby again wondered about the accuracy of the assumption, but the underlying vibe that Stacy had experienced something similar before made him willing to follow the trail of blood. The two walked into the forest, uncertain what they would find. Dasher could very well be dead, but at least they would know. If he wasn't dead, they needed to help him and he needed to help this country, which, by virtue of mathematics, meant they needed to help this country. For once in Kibby's life, he felt like someone.

Somewhere in the Forest, Montana, United States

"You don't talk much do you, Serone?" Dasher asked, as they wandered through the forest to claim revenge on the two remaining mercenaries that had kidnapped Duke.

Serone suggested heading to the highway so they could hitch a ride back to civilization and regroup, but he had been promptly ignored as they ventured deeper into the forest. In reality, Serone was quite talkative. He was an eclectic man with interests that covered the spectrum of potential conversation topics. The past few days had made Serone a shell of a man though; the combination of Dasher's misinformed interpretations of the world combined with his insatiable bloodlust had rendered Serone more or less mute. Dasher considered Serone's suggestion to return to society, but something about being in these woods was making him feel alive again. A part of him really didn't want to return to the mundane reality that was his wife and kids. His characterless house in the suburbs. His daily anti-abortion rallies and dreams of starting his very own Joseph and the Amazing Technicolor

Dreamcoat-themed conversion therapy center. In many ways, he felt he didn't belong. Perhaps society did not need someone like Dasher anymore, and in his mind, he certainly didn't need it.

"You said it Duke," Serone lamely replied to Duke's suggestion that he was a quiet man.

"In some ways, we're kind of like Huck Finn and Tom Sawyer out here! Coupla kids and our zany hijinks," said a beaming Dasher trying to put the worrisome looking Serone at ease. The erroneous comparison only served to disturb Serone even further.

Dasher was still covered in mud and dirty as hell. The sound of soil disintegrating combined with the clamor of his clenched jaw and grinding teeth added to the serene noises of nature surrounding them. Thankfully, he opted to put his clothes back on, but he had zipped the bottoms off his convertible pant shorts. Noting audibly to Serone that he never thought he would see the day, but it was hot as all get out. Dasher was a man of severe modesty and the capri length pants he zipped into were in direct betrayal of that modesty. Nonetheless, he prayed on it and God had given him the green light to expose his shins and calves to the world. The sweet Lord was generous that day.

The two continued on their hunt, as Dasher tried to keep things light and cheer Serone up by doing things like tipping Serone's hat off with his loaded shotgun, discussing the dangers of female empowerment and explaining the objective falsehood of other religions.

145

Serone found his eyes wandering directly into the sun's glow, hoping that it would burn through his retinas, enter his brain and eventually put him into a permanent coma. Serone fantasized about collapsing and having his dissolved brain pour freely from his ears. He wondered if Dasher would notice or care.

Just as Serone's eyes were about to give, they came across an unusual sight. Dasher recognized the familiar, blue-collared shirt of the Christian icon that tried to kidnap him and murder his son only days earlier. Joel Oscreen stood, unnaturally still, by a river with a mild current. The sound of the river combined with the motionless beige mass was extremely unsettling. Dasher wondered if he was practicing a new homily technique and decided to watch from a distance to see if his intuition was correct. After several minutes of intense gazing, Dasher approached the man. Dasher was still uncertain whether or not he could kill this man, even after what he had done to his family. He was a man of God and nothing he did could change that.

"Oscreen, turn around!" shouted Dasher, pointing the shotgun at Oscreen's head. Oscreen remained motionless; his body maintained just enough firmness to stay upright.

"Turn around!" Dasher screamed again. Joel Oscreen didn't move.

Serone pushed Dasher's shotgun down and began instinctively walking forward in an almost surreal dream-like sequence. This was not the behavior of a ruthless mercenary; something was off. He approached Oscreen and put his hand on his shoulder. The shirt and underlying mass underneath felt like uncooked chicken breasts: slippery, pliable, and seemingly not human.

"Serone, what's happening over there? That must be one hell of a prayer!" Dasher yelled, lowering his shotgun and walking over to Serone and Oscreen.

Serone removed his hand from the shoulder of Oscreen and the body collapsed to the floor, crumbling as though it were boneless. Dasher and Serone stood there confused. They both wondered what the hell was going on. Even though the prior deaths had been inhuman and terrifying, at least Serone could wrap his head around the concept of murder. This was something his brain was not prepared to process.

"I think I have an idea, this is a known medical condition called prayer paralysis...it happens to people who regularly attend church Serone, not that you'd know," said Dasher. "When people would get like this during one of Father Tony's patented five-hour sermons back at my church in Rockford, we would re-baptize them in freezing cold water in an attempt to physically and spiritually awaken them," continued Dasher.

His childlike understanding of modern medicine was both heartwarming and terrifying. Though Serone knew the waters of the river would in no way rejuvenate the pile of stinking flesh before them, he let Dasher perform the ceremony out of pity and morbid curiosity. Serone was still wondering what had killed Oscreen and why he was left in

147

such a peculiar position. With nothing else to do, Serone saw no harm in letting Dasher attempt to revive the pastor by performing a baptism, even if he smelled as though he had been dead for hours.

Dasher marched the body into the water. It sagged in his arms like a wet sleeping bag. Oscreen's eyes and teeth had both fallen from his face, as did his finger and toenails. His fingers stretched limply towards the ground below. His tongue fell from his mouth and landed with a surprisingly loud wet thud at Dasher's feet, it flopped around nonchalantly before seeming to lose momentum and submitting itself for supper to a swarm of flies. Dasher went on, somehow unblinking at the revolting skin sack, and entered the water to prepare for his rejuvenating baptism.

"In the name of the father!" he said as he dunked the head under. When he pulled it up, it had completely disintegrated. All that was left was a ball of hair and a bundle of nerves. The rest of the corpse bled into the water creating a jigsaw puzzle of innards. The liquefied organs and dermis were taken with the current, immediately consumed by a horde of seagulls who lapped up the skin soup and instantly retched it back into the water. Serone followed suit. Dasher stared at the hair and nerves, rubbed them between his fingers and felt something hard in the middle of the human debris. Dasher held it up to Serone.

"What the hell is this Serone?" asked Dasher.

Serone looked closely at the item in Dasher's hand.

It appeared to be some type of microchip. He explained to Dasher that it was something generally found in computers.

"Are you saying that Joel Oscreen was a clone made by the Russians and implanted on U.S. soil with the sole task of killing and enslaving us all?" Dasher asked, making a rather unlikely diagnosis of the current situation. "Potentially..." Serone said, giving Dasher a hand out of the river. He was fascinated by Dasher's thought process and propensity towards virtually any conspiracy.

"I can't say for sure, but this microchip seemed to control Oscreen, and must have had some type of malfunction," continued Serone. "We need to find someone who can analyze this ASAP. Dasher, I implore you to head back into the city."

"It must have malfunctioned after it recognized he was a clone with an incorrect religious affiliation...cloning is a sin in the eyes of God, Serone. Didn't anyone ever tell you how babies are born? And I'll head back after I've killed that horse scientist and not a minute before," Dasher replied sharply.

"I'll decide who heads back into the city," said an oddly horse-like voice that came from underneath the shadow of the giant oak tree. "I've been watching this whole time. Hand over the microchip," Hisan said, emerging into full eyesight of Serone and Dasher. Dasher ambled up the bank and towards Hisan, who had his AK47 pointed at him and Serone.

"Walk the microchip over here slowly Dasher. I told Popov not to use these cheap pieces of crap for a mission as important as this," continued Hisan.

Dasher instantly recognized the name Popov again and noted the term 'cheap pieces of crap'. Cheaply made…pieces of crap…this stunk like the Russians, that much was for sure. Serone, on the other hand, was wondering if the two's journey had finally come to an end. He was grateful that the trip was over in some ways. At least his time with Dasher had expired. A sense of calmness washed over him, knowing that soon enough, he would be dead and free from his self-constructed prison. If there was an afterlife, he hoped he would be sent to wherever Dasher was not.

"You really think it would be this easy...Hisan?" asked Dasher, smirking.

"Cool it with the psychobabble bullshit Dasher. Before long you and Serone will perish together and the United States will fall," replied Hisan.

"Nice try! I have a wife and kid, Hisan. Serone and I's relationship is strictly platonic!" stammered Dasher, completely misreading the situation and making everyone else wonder if he did hold some deep-seeded feelings for Serone.

"Reach into my right cargo pocket Hisan, and don't you dare get handsy in there!" said Dasher. "Don't worry, I won't bite," Dasher continued, making a snapping motion with his teeth.

Hisan was confused by the suggestion. Something inside him told him he had to find out what was in that pocket. Every fiber of his being told him to spend an entire round on these two goons, but something froze his finger on the trigger. He wondered why he was suddenly paralyzed, obsessed with the prospect of what was hidden in Dasher's pocket, even though it was likely a family portrait taken at JC Penny of him and his wife posing fully nude as Adam and Eve. Then he heard a noise coming from the pocket Dasher had told him to check. A screaming that did not sound quite human. Hisan's mind instantly flashed back to the hybrid mini horse slaughter in the desert all those years back. The face of one particular mini horse hybrid staring back at him after its head had been torn off by a wolf became clear as day in his mind. He yelled back in agony at whatever was screaming in Dasher's pocket. Serone covered his ears and rocked back and forth on the ground.

"Goddamnit Dasher! Did you record the slaughter you limp dicked fool?!" Hisan demanded, cautiously approaching Dasher.

"Do you take me for some kind of pervert Hisan? I am a God-fearing Christian, remember? That type of thing would never cross my mind," Dasher snarled, reaching slowly into his pocket and extracting a small television that appeared to be live streaming whatever was causing the

151

ear-bleeding commotion.

Hisan picked up the handheld screen and cradled it in his hands. He began to weep instantly. One of his human mini-horse hybrids hung suspended over what appeared to be an oversized garbage disposal. The screaming subsided; it seemed the lights flashing on the camera recording it had only startled the horse. The hybrid appeared actually pleasant enough, well-fed, and content. Hisan, however, looked again at the several TRX ropes that suspended the horse over what resembled a makeshift, oversized garbage disposal. Hisan collapsed to one knee momentarily. He was still holding his gun, but simply overcome with too much emotion to even stand.

"Where the hell is this Dasher? Make no mistake, you're dying today, but that horse does not deserve to, you coward!" Hisan shouted at the top of his lungs, nearly crushing the tiny television in his massive and extremely hairy hands.

"Your precious hybrid horse won't die if you play your cards right Hisan. I'm not a spineless piece of human filth like you," said Dasher smugly. "After the incident in the desert, I found one of the horses roaming around helplessly, picking the final meat off the bones of his brothers. I lured it in with an Omaha steak and captured it. It has been suspended over that garbage disposal in my basement for the last several years waiting for this very moment Hisan.

I am a man of extreme preparedness you see... I've made

152

a lot of enemies and I'll be damned if they think they're punching my ticket to heaven."

Hisan looked at Serone, desperately trying to understand what was going on. His tear-filled eyes sought any morsel of sympathy. They fell upon the surprisingly indifferent face of Mikel Serone. His face appeared similar to an old piece of waterlogged driftwood, an emotionless log simply abiding by the current of the body of water it resides in until eventually succumbing to the weight of the water and sinking completely. The most he could muster was a small shoulder shrug; the incident had actually passed without much thought given everything else that had transpired over the last few days.

Creating an elaborate death trap for the sole purpose of holding a lab-created, temperamental human-horse hybrid hostage based on the remote possibility that a scientist who had escaped a decade ago would someday seek revenge was almost downright predictable. Serone imagined the number of man hours that had gone into creating the device, not to mention feeding and caring for the horse, ensuring that, at a bare minimum, it was alive just enough to drop into the disposal and cause a mental breakdown for anyone unfortunate enough to witness it.

Hisan looked closer at the video. He noticed an enormous collection of Precious Moments statues in a glass enclosure in the corner of the room. When they initially kidnapped Dasher, there was a distinct, bordering on unsettling, amount of Precious Moments statues littered throughout the house. For an adult, a single Precious Moments statue

153

is troubling; the several dozen he saw strewn about the Dasher household made him question whether he wanted to actually pursue this lunatic at all. The statues' giant eyes were black pools that consumed the sanity of their owners. "That's your house Dasher. Your obsession with large-eyed commemorative statues gave you up. Now I can blow your head off and live happily ever after with my creation," Hisan said with the vigor of the crazy old bastard who just achieved checkmate on a piss-soaked outdoor chess table in New York.

A toothless smile formed on Dasher's face, his lips stretching for what seemed to be an eternity. The mud on his face cracked and fell onto the leaves below like crusted snot falling from the congested nostril of a balding and sickly co-worker onto a worn keyboard. The other men present wondered what was going through his mind. Maybe this was just the face you made when you were going to die. Maybe Dasher was fantasizing about the homily given at his funeral. Perhaps he simply had enough of everything he despised in this world - all of the bitching and whining, the millennial snowflake bull crap. Maybe he was finally ready for some peace and quiet. Then he spoke.

"You really think I would be that careless Hisan? You can kill me if you want, but when you do, the horse is jammed right into that industrial-grade wood chipper," said Dasher.

Hisan thought about what Dasher had just said and assumed it to be the last act of a desperate man. Nothing more than a bluff. Though given the precarious situation and his entire world at stake, Hisan had to entertain the thought that Dasher was somehow capable of killing that horse hybrid all these miles away.

"Spill it Dasher. There's no sense in playing coy you little pissant," said Hisan.

"For once in your entire miserable existence, you're right Hisan. You've wasted enough of all of our time," said Dasher snickering. "Serone, come over here."

Serone followed Dasher's erect finger, which pointed to a spot directly behind him. Dasher pulled Serone close and whispered something in his ear. Serone sullenly shook his head; apparently whatever was said was disagreeable. Dasher pulled him in once more - the verbal lashing was apparent even as a whisper. The awkward exchange between the two went on for several minutes. Hisan considered killing them both right there, but his curiosity got the better of him, and he let the two quietly negotiate without interruption. Finally, Serone wrapped his arms around Dasher's neck and began slowly choking him out. "What the hell is going on!" Hisan shouted at the bizarre occurrence taking place before his bloodshot eyes. Serone once again shrugged as his grip tightened around Dasher's neck. Dasher was growing limper by the second. His eyes were wide open staring at Hisan, his face turning blue. He seemed eager for unconsciousness to set in.

As white foam of spit began to form on Dasher's mouth and blood vessels burst in his eyes, Hisan heard something

coming from the miniature TV - a cranking sound.
He frantically picked up the TV, fighting the urge to watch
Dasher's seizing body as it went to sleep by way of
Serone's strangling. The crane that held the hybrid horse
was, in fact, lowering. Hisan cried out helplessly at what he
was seeing, not totally sure of what was taking place within
the confines of the cramped screen. Then he noticed a tiny
heart monitor in the corner of the display; the crane was
lowering in direct correspondence with Dasher's heart rate.
As Dasher's rate slowed, the machine dropped the horse
closer to its gruesome death. He looked up and Dasher
was completely out, laying on the ground and drooling all
over himself.

"Wake him up! Wake him up you idiot!" screamed Hisan,
pointing the gun at Serone.

Serone abided by splashing some cold water, which
coincidentally had the remains of Joel Oscreen's skin and
some seagull vomit, on Dasher's face. His lifeless body
rested for several additional seconds, followed by an
enormous gurgling from his pants. He blinked both eyes
open and took a colossal inhale of air, coughing several
times violently. He looked at Hisan and grinned once
more.

"By now you've figured it out. Kill me and the horse is
dead. I blew Terry's entire college fund, took out a second
mortgage and pawned Stacy's wedding ring to create this
device and the look on your face is making it entirely
worth it," said Dasher. "You better take off Hisan. That

crying horse ain't gonna save itself," continued Dasher, knowing he had bettered his rival this time around. Hisan backed up. Holding the gun pointed at the two men, he took several steps back into the confines of the forest before finally turning around and sprinting away, eventually disappearing into the thick woods. The love he had for those animals trumped the hatred he had for Dasher. He had to find his prized horse, nurse it back to health, and give it the life he always wanted but could never have.

"I gotta say Dasher, that took an unexpected turn. I guess I'm just glad to be alive," Serone said, rubbing the back of his head in complete astonishment. "It's not every day you see something like that," continued Serone.

"If I had it my way...this would be every day," Dasher replied ominously.

13 Family Reunion and the Death of a Dream

Somewhere in the Forest,
Montana,
United States

Patrick Kibby and Stacy Dasher happened upon a
depraved looking campsite after walking for some time.
The site itself reeked of kidnapping mercenaries and
contained a heavily used looking real doll, which slightly
resembled the bastard cousin of an indiscernible reality TV
star, a s'more making kit and several sizeable piles of feces
covered in excitable maggots. There was no actual fire, but
instead, a Microsoft Surface Pro displaying a seasonal
holiday fire screensaver. The digital rendering of flames
and presence of a Microsoft tablet made the campsite
seem that much more unwell. Kibby put his infinity scarf
around his face in an attempt to mask the smell with the
cologne he purchased at his most recent visit to Trunk
Club. He pulled his Rob Kardashian fedora deeper around
his scalp, hoping to cover as much of his skin as possible
from the depravity at hand.

Stacy noticed white powder caking on the plastic exterior
of the real doll, she licked the substance and confirmed it
was cocaine, though she explained to Kibby that is was
"incredibly stepped on" and did not pursue any further
consumption of the rest of the powder stuffed into varying
nooks and crevices of the sex doll. Nor did she elaborate
on the description of the cocaine, which had left Kibby
visibly mystified. Overall, the camp looked abandoned,
which comforted Kibby, but he wondered why. Why was
the twisted dwelling set up in the first place? Maybe it was
just several men succumbing to carnal urges around the

warm glow of a fake fire on a Microsoft tablet likely bought at a H.H. Gregg closeout sale. He tried not to think about what had happened here in the nights prior. Nevertheless, his mind ultimately conjured up the image of several nude men getting blackout drunk and hastily passing around a decomposing real doll, ravenous and overwhelmed by the romantic glow of the artificial fire and endless stream of vodka. The tablet illuminated the excess of fluids.

He picked up the dripping tablet, stirring it awake. The wetness was unnerving. Kibby instantly wiped his hands on his pants, praying that it was merely urine. It automatically connected to a 2G Cricket Wireless network, which Kibby did not even know existed. Absolutely no one used Cricket Wireless, so whatever was happening on this tablet was either so inconsequential the users did not care about service, or it was so top secret they wanted to avoid government listening by using a network that was promoted during daytime television and was preceded by several advertisements for personal injury lawyers. He glanced over at Stacy Dasher, who had produced a magnifying glass out of nowhere and was furiously examining the excrement while having an argument with herself over whether or not Cecil the Lion killed Kurt Cobain. Kibby returned to the familiar blue glow of the screen. The same glow that had created an insatiable orgy of worms in his brain who were perpetually seeking orgasm by means of the blue light, who were impregnating themselves with limitless, heaving fistfuls of stinking content and who were quickly becoming a substitute for a viable personality.

He noticed three tabs open. One tab was a halfway filled out form for a structured settlement with J.G. Wentworth. The presence of the site itself and the inability to complete a standard web form suggested a transcendent incompetence and questionable financials. The second tab was a confirmation message for a successfully ordered adult-sized Minions costume. Strike two in Kibby's brain, as anyone over the age of five who still liked Minions was as equally harmful to society as a group of mercenaries attempting a governmental coup. Kibby opened the third tab and noticed several hundred recordings with varying date and time stamps. He started with the most recent recording. The recording was more bizarre than Kibby could have ever anticipated. It sounded like someone practicing a speech for their local Toastmasters chapter in which they attempted to make an impassioned speech in favor of naming the Epcot Center in Orlando, Florida an official wonder of the world.

The speech was poorly written and ripe with stuttering, garbling and brutal mouth breathing. Kibby hoped that whoever had recorded this would die before they ever got a chance to unleash it on the world. Although, Stacey had picked up several parts of the speech and nodded in thoughtful agreement especially at the speaker's point regarding Epcot Center's resident barbershop quartet, The Dapper Dans, and their unrivaled, well-conceived and articulated harmonizing ability.

He selected the next recording and found something entirely different. Two men, one Russian, one seemingly Middle Eastern, discussing a plot to ruin the United States government and enslave its people in detail. Kibby's face lost the little color it had. If the recording on this Microsoft Surface Pro was even remotely true, they were in a lot of trouble. The country was already weakened and its constituents were desperate for change. The prospect of being enslaved by a Russian with a debilitating drinking problem and his army of cheap celebrity replicas would probably garner a standing ovation if it were pitched correctly during one of the many asinine debates, especially if they got an endorsement from the coveted Vapers of America booster club, which had gained substantial power after the President popularized the vile habit.

Kibby's biggest concern was their mention that the President was a willing participant in all of this. Maybe he was not involved at the birth of this revolution, but he was certainly involved now. The recording referred to a time and location where the President would formally submit his allegiance to Vladimir Popov. If the President had his tongue inserted deeply and firmly in the frozen center of this shit casserole, Kibby didn't know what to do next. Who else had taken a drink from Popov's tainted bottle of hooch? Had the police and military also suckled vodka from Popov's chapped nipples? Were they also drunk off the tainted breast milk flowing freely from Popov's reddened udders? Kibby thought about whom he could trust and realized the answer was absolutely no one. Stacy Dasher was going ballistic on a squirrel who she thought resembled Bernie Sanders, so Kibby was left alone in thought. Stacy caught the squirrel and beat it to death on a nearby rock.

He put the tablet down and began to cry. For the first time in his life, he couldn't worm his way out of something. The country was doomed and there was nothing he could do about it. He could publish another article, but he knew it would not take off in time. The meeting was tomorrow and he was on the outs with his editor after the first Duke Dasher list he published. Just when he thought all hope was lost, he saw two men walking towards them.

Somewhere in the Forest,
Montana,
United States

Stacy looked up and immediately began crying. The man who she learned to tolerate after all of those years was alive and well. The marriage she had grown content with over the last decade, and was loosely held together by a child they both resented, had been resurrected from the dead. Though part of her longed for Dasher to be dead, which would be the catalyst for her to finally change; she was still oddly relieved that he was alive. She had grown accustomed to the oppressive nature of their relationship and fear of the unknown ultimately surpassed general malaise. Simply existing until finally giving out and being celebrated with a sparsely attended funeral is the most anyone can really expect - Stacy Dasher was no different. She fantasized about an affordable coffin and a continental breakfast for the few people unfortunate enough to mourn her insignificant life. Countless years of personal growth, creative endeavors and emotional hardship distilled into a cinnamon apple Danish being gummed by a distant relative.

She ran serpentine towards Duke Dasher and embraced him, sobbing heavily into his blood-soaked shirt.

"You look like crap Duke," said Stacy.

"You should see the other guys," Dasher replied with a chuckle.

Serone thought back on the defiled corpses littered like pieces of bothersome waste in the woods and objected to the suggestion. The three walked back to the campsite where Kibby remained glued to the tablet, struggling to digest the entirety of what he had discovered. Stacy Dasher looked like an entirely different woman upon returning, both physically and mentally. He watched her transform in front of his eyes, morphing from someone who, just hours earlier, pulled the teeth from an unconscious stranger and tied them to a cross bought from Skymall to a charming American sweetheart. Dasher noticed the look of dismay on Kibby's face and spoke with the quiet voice of an angry dad.

"Wives, submit yourselves to your own husbands as you do to the Lord. For the husband is the head of the wife as Christ is the head of the church, his body, of which he is the Savior. Now, as the church submits to Christ, so also wives should submit to their husbands in everything," Dasher said, with the same devout cluelessness as an aging, out-of-touch priest wrestling with dementia.

Serone and Kibby looked at Stacy for some type of objection, given how backward the statement was, but she remained quiet. The grin that she had been trained her entire life to maintain was tattooed on her paralyzed face, repressing a lifetime of feelings.

"Duke, I don't thi…" started Serone. A wave of relief hit Kibby's face, who was terrified to object to the psychotic ramblings.

"Ephesians 5:22," Dasher replied with a prideful tear in his eye and a slight snicker. Just stating the verse it came from in the Bible was enough to completely kill any thoughtful conversation and Dasher knew it. Absolutely no one messed with Ephesians. Dasher's beliefs and views trumped those around him. After all, shouldn't the direct extension of God himself be able to win an argument about the treatment of women with a verse from a book written several thousand years ago? Kibby spoke up, deciding to wade into the microwaved bathwater that swished freely in Dasher's skull.

"Sir, I don't think we've met. Patrick Kibby," he said, offering Dasher a cowardly, trembling salute.

"At ease cadet," said Dasher as he gave Kibby a condescending pat on the forehead. "You've done well so far. What happened to all of your teeth?"

"Stacy pulled them after she knocked me out, sir," replied Kibby with his now prevalent lisp.

"Atta girl," said Dasher, patting Stacy on the shoulder. She blushed at the compliment, much to the dismay of Kibby.

"First things first. There's something I need to take care of," announced Dasher. Serone and Kibby looked coyly at each other, assuming Dasher would dip and kiss Stacy and celebrate the reuniting of their family. Maybe a moment of humanism in someone who, up to that point in the journey, had been anything but. Instead, Dasher began furiously grinding his teeth and straining his neck. Every rope-like vein became completely visible as though he had no skin at all. His mouth began foaming once more; every muscle contracted in unison and Dasher collapsed to the ground. Serone and Kibby weren't sure what to do. They immediately began searching the campsite for a First Aid kit. Stacy commenced a booming countdown, starting at 20 and counting backward.

The other two men stopped what they were doing to absorb the insanity around them. Duke's corpse lay perfectly still on the ground; the only movement was a steady drip of blood slithering from both nostrils. Stacy's count was oddly patriotic. Her eyes were unblinking; her voice was unwavering, as though she had been training for this moment for her entire life. She seemed to realize her purpose on this earth during the fervid countdown that accompanied her inert husband. The men feared what would happen when she inevitably reached zero. When Stacy reached the number five, the men heard an unpleasant clicking sound coming from the pocket of her Wrangler jeans. Stacy reached into the jeans and brandished a military-grade Taser, yanking it out and hoisting it above her head like Excalibur being pried from its enormous boulder. When she hit zero, she slammed the Taser into the forehead of Duke Dasher.

Kibby puked bile onto the shoulder of Serone, who instinctively pissed himself. Dasher sat up and scratched his head. He tilted his neck both ways and everyone present could hear an audible bone cracking. Dasher then grinned at Serone, a calculated grin...with someone extremely nefarious lurking behind those otherwise virtuous lips. The gravity of what had just occurred hit Serone like a ton of bricks.

"Dasher, you didn't. You couldn't have," Serone said, attempting to hold back tears.

"You bet your ass I did Serone," replied Dasher. "An eye for an eye and your other eye and the rest of your family as the Bible says."

"What is going on?" cried Kibby, overwhelmed by the traumatic event that had just occurred.

"Duke spent the entirety of our life savings on a device that hoisted a human-mini horse hybrid over an enormous garbage disposal. He took the hybrid from a facility in Iraq with the assumption that the evil scientist who worked at the lab would someday attempt revenge for the slaughter of the rest of the herd. Knowing that he may not be able to push the button and drop the mini hybrid to its horrific death, Dasher installed a heart rate monitor in himself. The engineering behind it is actually quite impressive. If his heart completely stops, the horse is plummeted into the grinding gears and poured into a bottle of Elmer's glue," said Stacy in a matter-of-fact tone.

"My counting back from twenty ensured that the horse was completely ground into oblivion; we spent most of our honeymoon rehearsing this exact scenario. Once the deed was done, I shocked Duke back to life with this head Taser," continued Stacy, flicking the on switch of the Taser a few more times.

Kibby vomited up more bile. His abs ached from heaving so much. Dasher's misinterpretation of an outdated Bible verse had gone more or less unnoticed as the two men considered the prospect of doing this drill on a honeymoon and then actually executing it in real life. The amount of time and energy spent preserving that horse was downright astonishing.

"Was that really necessary?" screamed Serone. "The man said he was going to live peacefully with that horse!"

"Is protecting our country necessary? Is carrying out God's will necessary?" sneered Dasher. "That horse was the last bargaining chip I had; I did what I had to do. We won't be bothered by Hisan anymore. When he comes across that glue bottle, he will be broken."

Hisan would absolutely be broken. Serone had to give him that. In some ways, Dasher's ability to drive his enemy to the brink and then push them further was an impressive feat. Serone was happy that he wasn't on the other end of this ruthless maniac who had truly transformed into his nickname God Hand. Stacy Dasher stood there giggling.

"If that device had gone unused Duke, boy, I would have

been awfully sad!" said Stacy. "But you knew all along; somehow, you always know Duke!"

In Rockford, Illinois, a man was desperately trying to save the only love of his life.

**Rockford,
Illinois,
United States**

Hisan kicked down the door to Dasher's house. He hoped he had made it in time. He barreled down the basement stairs, tripping over a Precious Moments statue and falling directly on his back. The popping sound he heard was sickening and when he tried to move, his legs were not functioning. No time to worry about being paralyzed now; he could still ride this horse into the sunset, or so he thought. He crawled furiously towards the machine, which occupied most of the basement. The sheer size and complexity of the contraption was a testament to how consumed with madness Dasher must have been. The room was mostly black, but the machine still glistened, even in the dark; it was meticulously clean.

Hisan scrambled for a light switch, using his arms to propel the rest of his limp body across the floor. Anything to let him see his horse once more.

After finding the switch, he flailed helplessly at its base for several moments before painfully clawing his way up. His fingertips bloodied from the steep, unrelenting brick wall.

He flicked the light switch hoping to see those doughy eyes staring back, full of hope and wonder.

Instead, he saw a tattered rope and harness, chewed to bits by the grinding gears below, which were still grinding as machines do. The sound of metal on metal suggested they had eaten through the flesh and bone hours ago. The whirring sound persisted relentlessly, bludgeoning Hisan's eardrums. Maybe it escaped? Maybe the horse figured out a way to undo the harness before it dropped. Yet, he knew in his heart the hybrid horse was far too stupid to achieve something like that, especially after having lived contently hovering above those whirring gears for several years.

He looked at the rubber hose that had been crudely fashioned into the tub where the gears turned. He saw it had previously been connected to an empty bottle of Elmer's glue, but because of the force of the contents spewing from the machine, it had since tipped over. Dasher had clearly neither understood how paste was made nor anticipated the sheer volume of pulpy guts the hybrid would render once blended. The mess around the tipped bottle was substantial. Hisan cried one last time. He had spent his entire life trying to create a legacy for himself, something that would outlast his time on this earth. He desperately sought some form of immortality. The prospect of death frightened him, knowing that his daily toil would be instantly forgotten once he passed. Friends and families may reminisce from time to time, but otherwise, the earth would be indifferent to his minor contributions. In his effort to create that legacy, he made something he truly loved, something that transcended his

170

desire for remembrance. He had sought revenge, but after seeing his life's work haphazardly splattered over a tipped Elmer's glue bottle, he lost his will to live.

He crawled up the rope that hovered above the contraption and before he dropped himself in, he considered the fortune of having ever created something. Though the creation was short-lived and tragic and led him to his current suspended position over an enormous garbage disposal built for the sole purpose of destroying all that he loved, it had been realized; and for that, he felt indebted to the universe. Knowing he would never create something with so much beauty again, he lowered himself in and met the same demise as his masterpiece. The gears ate through his skin and bone with ease, weakly sputtering his remains on top of his hopes and dreams, which already stained the basement carpet. A forgettable drying crust in a basement in Rockford Illinois.

14 Operation Diesel Fist…Again

Somewhere in the Forest,
Montana,
United States

Kibby held the tablet in front of the group at the campsite. They all paused momentarily, thinking they heard the distant scream of a broken man a thousand miles away, but ultimately agreed that it was probably just a group of blue-winged warblers, which were common in that region of Montana and known to sound like a man slowly lowering himself into a death trap after losing the only thing he ever loved. He played the recordings for the team who listened carefully, save Dasher who was furiously burning the remains of all of the pornographic magazines lying around. Dasher had made a fire using a healthy amount of kindling and a match from his Vatican souvenir.

"And you didn't want me to buy that relic…" Dasher said to Stacy. "If I hadn't bought it, we'd all be dead right now and you would be feeling pretty dumb."

Serone and Kibby exchanged a brief glance suggested that each of them had experienced their own version of Dasher hell.

The recordings unveiled the entire depth of the sinister agreement between an alcoholic Russian spy and the President of the United States. It revealed the massive network of cloning facilities that doubled as Spencer's Gifts, but for some reason, every patron was too stupid or careless to notice, distracted by electric orbs, naked lady shrimp de-veiners, and alien-themed blacklight weed posters. The fact that celebrities were being cloned and, at a certain point, would be turned into Russian soldiers in charge of instilling order under the newly-formed communist regime, and no one seemed to notice or care, was a true testament to how completely aloof the country was.

All it took was the flip of a switch by Popov and his entire army would be turned into killing machines. It was a deal co-signed by the devil himself. If the recordings were accurate, in two days, the citizens of the United States would be the third unwilling member in this unholy devil's threesome.

"You hear that, Dasher?" asked Serone. Dasher threw the real doll into the fire and it erupted in flames.

"I heard it, and in some ways, I already knew. Remember my oddly specific prediction when we found the microchip in the melted corpse of Joel Oscreen?" asked Dasher.

"The only thing I hate more than celebrities is celebrity clones. Life should only be conceived by a man and a woman, with the man having the more important role in the conception process and the woman more or less just being a duffle bag for the man's seed. Once you start bringing in science and Petri dishes, you mess with everything God wanted for us. Clones are worse than abortions."

Kibby and Serone stole a knowing glance at each other, recognizing they had in fact experienced their own version of Dasher family hell. Serone thought back and remembered the prophecy he had told. He thought back to what Stacy previously said: Duke always knows - except in cases of having informed or rational opinions about most of the things happening in the world, but in this very particular, singular circumstance, Duke did know. Kibby looked helpless as ever.

"Duke...what do we do?" asked Kibby.

Dasher walked over to Kibby and ripped the tablet from his smooth wet hands, which had never seen a day of hard work. His buttermilk palms were barely capable of holding anything; they were built for absolutely nothing but resting on a keyboard. Dasher looked at the tablet for a moment while everyone else brimmed with anticipation as to what Dasher would do. He held something that could change the entire landscape of the country, and by extension the world, in his hands. Something that had the potential to alter the lives of virtually every person living in the United States. Something that, if not handled appropriately, would plummet the country into poverty and enslavement by way of cloned celebrities and sketchy Russians.

Kibby looked down and realized he had bitten clean through his nails. His fingers were bleeding profusely, but his focus remained on the unchanging face of Duke Dasher. Serone looked at Stacy, who looked at Kibby, who looked back at Stacy, their faces drenched in sweat, their breath stale and gamey.

Dasher looked up to the sky, muttered something incomprehensible, and threw the tablet into the fire. "Duke, no!" yelled Serone.

Kibby collapsed onto the ground and folded on top of himself, shaking uncontrollably. Stacy continued to giggle. Dasher stared into the fire; the flames reflected in his pupils. After several seconds, Kibby came to and scrambled towards the fire. Serone immediately grabbed him, even though he knew it was too late.

"That was everything, Duke! Everything we had to prove out this terrible conspiracy was on that tablet!" Kibby said in a voice so shrill it was barely audible to the rest of the group.

"If we're gonna do this, we're gonna do it my way," Dasher calmly replied, cracking his knuckles. Serone shuddered. Up to that point, Duke Dasher's way had been a perpetually escalating series of the worst things he had ever and probably would ever see in his life.

"Have you guys ever heard about the mission that got me honorably discharged from my special forces unit?" asked Dasher, waiting for an immediate affirmative from the rest of the group. The mission was legendary and essentially folklore at this point. It even lived in some history books, favoring that event over things like World Wars and the entire Civil Rights Movement.

"You mean Operation Diesel Fist?" asked Kibby, followed by an audible gulp.

"You bet your ass, kid," said Dasher, who paired his enthusiastic words with a massive fist pump. "For those of you who don't remember, I sawed the face off of a rebel leader...and then, wearing his face, I convinced all of the insurgent rebels to take their own lives. You see, getting the face off was relatively easy but re-apply..."

"We are all very aware of Operation Diesel Fist, I don't think it requires any additional discussion," interrupted Serone, mercifully saving everyone from another gruesome reenactment. "How is that situation at all relevant to you burning all the evidence of collusion between the President and Popov we had?" Before he finished the question, he already knew the answer.

"That's right Serone. I'll be paying Popov a little visit. His face is mine," replied Dasher. "Once I have that, I catch the President red-handed, mano-a-mano. None of this second-hand recording crap. I want the President to lie to my face...which will be in turn behind Popov's face..." Dasher said trailing off absently.

No one offered any better ideas, so it was settled. Dasher pulled out his Motorola Razr and pressed a number for speed dial. Serone wondered why Dasher hadn't used the phone hours ago when they were being hunted, but decided he better not mention it. Ultimately, it did not matter. There was still the question of getting there in time for the meeting or before Popov got drunk enough to activate the kill switch, which would turn the clones into an unstoppable, murderous rebel force.

"Watley? Send her down," Dasher said grittily into the phone. It was the voice of someone who had smoked a million cigarettes over the course of their lifetime, even though he had never smoked even one. Out of nowhere, a hulking drone descended from the clouded skies and landed by the weary group of four.

"You had a drone watching us this whole time?" asked Serone, at this point, absolutely beside himself.

"Never leave home without it," Dasher grinned without providing any more explanation on the specifics of having 24/7 drone surveillance. "Watley is a good man," was all he offered. Behind his words, he knew Watley's life was in shambles ever since he took up the service of 24/7 Duke Dasher drone monitoring.

His wife and kids had left him and he was in terrible physical health. His feet were consumed in gout and his diet consisted almost exclusively of Monster Energy, gas station sex pills and shellfish. Monitoring Dasher's every action had definitely taken its toll. However, Watley considered it an honor to provide Dasher with the rarely-needed service. It was moments like these Watley cherished in life - not anniversaries or graduations, but protecting another man during even the most mundane of Saturdays. Dasher had also promised him immediate entry into heaven, which was certainly a perk Watley could not pass up.

Dasher approached the drone and petted it like a wild stallion. Running his hands slowly across its steel mane.

"Easy girl, easy," he said aloud to it, though the drone was quite still and needed no calming. Dasher beckoned the rest of the group over to him; they walked over with some hesitancy. "We need to get to Washington, D.C. to meet Popov, and ole Sally is going to get us there," explained Dasher, again stroking the smooth paneling of the drone.

"Dasher, I think the rest of us can stay behind, maybe catch a little shut-eye. It's been a long few days," offered Serone. He looked around at the others for approval and got it immediately.

"Nonsense Serone. I wouldn't do this thing without my dream team," said Dasher, pulling several cords with attached carabiners from the ski-like landing gear that had allowed the drone to land safely in the woods.

"Dasher, I hope you're not suggesting we ride this thing..." Kibby said apprehensively.

"Like Jesus and the donkey, Kibby...without the palm leaves," said Dasher, another eye-stinging joke landing tiredly on the rest of the groups' ears. Serone began slowly walking backward, hoping to hit the cover of the forest before Dasher noticed anything amiss.
Unfortunately for him, Dasher was trained to see virtually every detail of every scenario.

"Afraid of heights Serone? Not to worry, this thing will hit the speed of sound and you'll likely blackout almost instantly. Your lifeless body will be nothing more than a fleshy wind chime at that point," said Dasher as he acted out what Serone would look like once he was forced into unconsciousness by the speed of the drone.

The visual did very little to calm Serone's nerves. That settled it, the team was going. Dasher paused and counted the team over once more. Though numbers were not always his strong suit, as math oftentimes lead to larger sins, he noticed that something was off.

"Stacy? We're one short..." said Dasher.

"Terry will be fine in the car Duke! You worry too much!" replied Stacy.

"Yeah, but you think I want to deprive my boy of his first drone ride, learning how to cut the face off of some Russian piece of shit, saving the country and getting the girl?" said Dasher, proudly massaging Stacy's shoulders. The two agreed that Terry needed to witness this and, as if a message had been sent from God, when they looked up, they saw Terry wandering aimlessly in the field.

"Terry! I told you not to leave the car. What the hell are you doing out here!" screamed Stacy.

"Hey, don't fault the kid. He's got his old man's sense of adventure and some good ole fashioned blood lust, right boy?" asked Dasher hopefully. Terry stood completely still, uncertain how to answer either question.

"See there! He nodded, Stacy! I always told you he'd grow up to be just like me," Dasher said to the unmoving child. "Well, we should get a move on in that case."

Duke began buckling the team into the drone, which would fly them directly to Washington D.C. The drone looked rather poorly made and still had a tag on it from RadioShack; Dasher noted he would likely return it after the mission was up. He advised the team to be very careful because any dents or scratches and the warranty was voided. Three of them were uncomfortably strapped in and ready to go. Terry was next and Duke would simply hold onto one of the skis. No need for a safety chord, his grip strength could use some challenging, he told them. As Dasher turned around to grab Terry, he noticed something sprinting at them in the distance.

15 Reality Celebrity Clone Wars

Somewhere in the Forest,
Montana,
United States

Whatever it was looked rabid, running violently and with purpose. Dasher looked at the rapidly approaching figure and noticed it was none other than Steve Harvley, another one of the countless daytime television show hosts with a hell of a mustache and teeth the same size and consistency of fingers. Unlike his rival counterpart, who looked exactly like him in most ways, this particular daytime television host wore a brutal hairpiece over his shining bald head. The piece was always crudely sewn on and hanging on for dear life on television, and it was no different now - the nutria hair toupee hung on for dear life as the clone tore down the hill.

"Dasher, what the hell is going on over there?" Kibby said anxiously.

"We got company," replied Dasher. "You know that clone that dissolved in my hands earlier? I think we got another one, and he doesn't look as happy as he does hosting the New Year's Eve ball drop."

"Popov must have started flipping the kill switch on these things already!" replied Kibby as he attempted to unhook himself unsuccessfully.

"Stay put Kibby, this won't take long," said Dasher as he went to fetch his shotgun.

When he turned around, several more C-list celebrity clones were tearing across the field. He wondered where the hell these things were coming from; they were approaching faster than he anticipated. The entire cast of the show Duck Franchise, along with the Property Siblings, were all descending upon them. He did not have time to unhook anyone. He fetched an enormous Desert Eagle 5.0 and handed it to poor little Terry Dasher; his hands disappeared behind the huge handle and trigger.

"Son, one day you will grow up and disappoint everyone; don't let that day be today," Dasher said to Terry, who looked up at him with his doughy eyes, barely able to hold the 50-caliber handgun in his trembling tiny hands.

"If you pull the trigger, the gun shoots. Aim for the whites of the eyes," said Duke, without advising much else in the way of gun safety, such as expected recoil or the emotional toll of murdering someone. The clones were now close enough to smell. That awful sulfurous smell filled the air and Duke hoisted his shotgun up, preparing for a barrage. Terry stood nonchalantly beside him, unable to grasp the gravity of the situation.

"On my signal Terry," said Duke. Terry's hands began visibly shaking. He used every ounce of energy and strength in his body to hoist the gun up to shoulder level.

"Up to this point in your life, you've been a burden to everyone you've ever met. Today you change that Terry. Today you become a man in the eyes of God, and by extension, me," continued Dasher in a terrible attempt to instill some confidence in the young soldier.

The clones were twenty-five yards away and closing fast. Dasher continued the hold position, refusing to budge an inch. The other three already strapped into the drone filled the air with terrified shrieking as they struggled to undo the harness Dasher had placed them in. The entire scene would have crumpled any normal man, let alone child, but Terry Dasher held the line with this dad. He did not have any other choice.

"Hold…..hold…..hold…NOW!" Duke yelled directly into Terry's ear. Both of the Dasher boys let one rip just as Steve Harvley and both of the Property Siblings were mere inches from where they stood.

Duke's shotgun blast ripped through the heads of both Property Siblings; their corpses went limp, but the momentum carried them several feet past Duke towards where the drone sat. The bodies slid and nudged into the foot of Kibby, who looked down and instantly threw up spastically, only adding to the mess that now inhabited the space below him. The clone's faces twitched furiously; they looked up at him and repeated the phrase 'help me' until spewing a skin-toned liquid all over Kibby and dying - an image that would later consume Kibby and ruin his life in the coming years.

Terry's bullet blasted through the torso of Steve Harvley, who also skidded right past the two onto the ground next to the drone. Dasher walked up and finished the job,

185

blowing an enormous hole through Steve Harvley's face as Terry looked on, his eyes tearing up.

"Darnit Terry. I told you to aim for the eyes!" said Duke disappointed. But after looking at the sad face of Terry, he added sympathetically, "But you did maim him! And your old man got another kill to add to his body count."

More clones were populating the field now and sprinting in the same manner as the group Duke and his son had just put down.

"Let's ride Terry!" Duke screamed as he picked Terry up and sprinted for the drone.

He strapped Terry in and grabbed one of the skis while simultaneously calling Watley and telling him to get them out of there. The clones were closing in quickly and Dasher wondered if this was where they would all die. He cursed Watley and thought that maybe he had picked the wrong man for the job. Just as Dasher began telling Watley that his cowardice was the reason his wife left him and there was no chance in hell he was getting into heaven, the drone slowly rose from the ground. Several clones were just below and reached up, clawing and biting at their ankles and legs. Stacy booted someone in the face, who might not have even been a clone, rather just one of the women on ABC's *The View*, knocking them back to the ground as the drone gained height. Although the drone was definitely not equipped to carry this many people, it left rather unceremoniously, slowly and painfully hauling the group of five towards Washington D.C. where the final showdown for the soul of the United States was set to take place.

**In the Air,
Somewhere,
United States**

The group of five hovered in silence for what seemed like forever. Dangling like sausages in a rarely visited butcher's shop window in Northern Indiana, they each tried to make sense of what had just happened in their own way. Virtually everything that had just unfolded was unprecedented and made them all question the future of the country and their place in the universe.

Being hastily strapped into a budget drone from RadioShack, bought and navigated by a man whose life seemed to be mentally and physically unraveling, did not help matters. The current circumstance forced everyone to reflect heavily on his or her own mortality. Except for Duke, who was still stewing about Terry's imperfect shot and the prospect of the country falling into the hands of a Russian clone army. The whir of the drone provided the soundtrack for their extremely uncomfortable ride to Washington, D.C.

"Hey Duke?" Kibby asked, finally breaking the oppressive silence. "You ever think that Terry is going to be permanently scarred and incapable of living a normal life after what just happened?"

Duke thought for a moment. "Disappointing your dad is a

burden that you'll carry with you forever. He knows he should have hit that shot better and though our relationship is severely damaged and we'll likely be emotionally distant until I'm in a hospital bed begging for his forgiveness, he'll get through it. Hell, I did," replied Dasher, ignoring the potential emotional impact of Terry being forced to shoot a celebrity clone at the ripe age of eight.

The odd specificity of the comment created a dismal sentiment inside Kibby in more ways than he could even comprehend. Dasher had just displayed, for the first time, a heartbreaking realization of emotional intelligence and his flippancy with which it was delivered sent Kibby into an existential crisis. Dasher chuckled at the prospect of a lifetime of confused resentment; love is not what kept families together. Respect, and the perpetual quest for validation, was.

"Ain't that right son!" yelled Dasher over the drone's engines. Terry looked blankly forward, perhaps unaware that a question had even been posed to him. Dasher reached out and tousled the hair of Terry's motionless head in an attempt to stir a reaction, but Terry's head didn't budge. It was impossible to tell if his brain could even remotely comprehend what had happened.

"Stacy, that was a heck of a boot! That thing's jaw fell clean off!" yelled Dasher.

"I'm not even sure that was a clone! It looked like someone from *The View* had just gotten lost in the woods and was looking for a lift to D.C.!"

The group offered a barely audible laugh, some of them opening their mouths, yet unsure if any noise came out. Somehow, the pitiless death of another potential clone did not seem that comical in the grand scheme of things. Dasher turned around and attempted to recreate the face of the clone who had seized and vomited all over Kibby. His face contorted violently and a blood vessel visibly blew in the middle of his forehead; he gasped for air as though a plastic bag covered his head.

Everyone politely offered the same grin, similar to that of a coworker exiting a bathroom stall after an embarrassingly long dump. Kibby and Serone exchanged glances, wondering if the man who had already seemed on the brink of a breakdown had finally snapped. They were quick to settle themselves though; reminiscing about the atrocities and ignorance committed up until this point, they realized he was as unchanging as ever.

The rest of the flight passed without incident.

16 Piss Stained Carpets at Tilted Kilt Bar & Grill

Goat Knuckle Inn,
Washington D.C.,
United States

Dasher checked the five of them in at a budget motel in
downtown D.C. called The Goat Knuckle Inn. The room
itself had been debated by Serone and Kibby, each of
whom maintained they should have separate rooms, but
Dasher ultimately won out and booked a single room for
all of them with two twin beds and a half bath. They
entered the room and Dasher went back to his endless well
of insufferable dad humor.

"Home sweet home," said Dasher walking across the
sticky carpeting towards a full ashtray and pile of old
needles. "You guys could probably use a little shut-eye. I
need a shower," said Dasher.

The rest of them agreed; they were drained, but the
sleeping arrangements seemed less than ideal. Terry curled
up in one bed almost immediately, and not wanting to stir
the kid, the other three climbed into the second twin bed
and attempted to sleep like a bundle of number two
pencils.

"Sorry about this Stacy," Kibby said, turning his head and
awkwardly looking at her.

"It's alright. Duke just wants us all to be safe," replied
Stacy, her arms firmly at her sides, trying to make herself
as small as humanly possible. The steam from Dasher's
shower poured into the tiny room, making it even damper

than it already was. Unfortunately, Dasher had also decided to unload several days' worth of berries and leaves he had been eating into the already brown water standing in the destitute toilet. The steam held this stench and carried it thoroughly throughout the room, creating a visible sweat on the lamp, television, and battered shades. The three lying in bed outside forced themselves into a restless slumber, seeking asylum from the oppressive stench.

Dasher stood in the shower contemplating all that had transpired over the past few days. He did not believe in soap, as it was made for Millennial vanity. Goddamn snowflakes and their hygiene, he thought as the freezing cold water poured over his body. Heated water was something else Dasher despised. It kneaded the soft, veal-like muscles of weak-minded snowflake cucks. He wondered if all of the hot water had been responsible for turning their once hardened skulls into pulverized oatmeal. They say that cold showers are reserved for psychopaths and serial killers, which Dasher respected more than either of the aforementioned variations of progressive youngsters. At least they stood for something. Though the shower was bitterly cold, Dasher's body was on fire; both his rage against changing times and Russia, in addition to the allergic reaction to whatever the hell Serone's mud concoction was, had his blood absolutely boiling. The freezing cold water hitting his skin made steam that quickly filled the entirety of the bathroom and poured out into the bedroom.

He instantly thought that the day had, without a doubt,

192

cracked his top two hundred strangest days, but wasn't sure where to place it. Maybe late hundreds, he thought, considering some of the other vile situations he had been forced to endure for the betterment of the country and mankind itself. He cherished the feeling of being needed again though, happy to have some purpose other than consumption. He wondered if he could ever adhere to the popular ideology of surviving to perpetuate an eternal advertisement of yourself. Could he exist solely to be lukewarm trough slop, fed to friends and family so they could avoid their own anxieties? Nibbling at morsels of feigned excitement and adventure until there was nothing left to give? Face-tuning one last perfect Instagram picture before dying alone in your favorite easy chair in complete solitude? He finished his shower and dressed again; it was time to meet Popov and save the country.

Dasher exited the bathroom quietly. The entire room was asleep, which was perfect. He did not want to involve them in the last leg of this mission. It was far too dangerous. Besides, he could not trust his idiot son, who only hours earlier had fumbled a perfect shot at a clone sprinting towards them at full speed. He had to do this one on his own, just like the good ol' days. He preferred that Terry see his dad wearing the face of another man, but ultimately thought better of it, given everything that had happened in the forest. Duke spiraled into a rare and lengthy bout of deliberation. His feeble mind attempted to dissect the complexities that were not so complex. Terry had gotten his first taste of blood via a cheaply made Russian celebrity clone, but he seemed more standoffish than usual. Maybe the pressure had gotten to him or

193

maybe he was too chicken shit to follow his dad's example like any respectable son.

On the other hand, maybe the little spineless coward was catching feelings as young people do nowadays. Duke was still somehow surprised that his son had not wanted to celebrate with a couple of root beer floats with his old man. He hoped that Terry was silently cherishing what he had done earlier. Turning it over in his mind repeatedly until he was completely numb - experiencing the numbness that Dasher's father had and his father before that. One could always hope. Dasher glided across the carpeting towards the door. He looked back once more on his family and one-sided friends. This could be the last time he ever saw them. He was ready to do anything for his country and his God, even if it meant dying. He closed the doors and walked to the parking lot where he elbowed the window out of a conveniently placed Dodge Charger. Dasher thanked the Lord that someone else at the motel was smart enough to be driving American. If there hadn't been an American car, he would have been walking. He peeled out of the parking lot and headed towards the location that Hisan and Popov had discussed.

Washington D.C.,
Tilted Kilt Pub & Eatery,
United States

Vladimir Popov sat at the fast-casual franchise restaurant he had acquired in a high stakes Texas Hold Em' tournament months earlier. The mercenaries should have been at the meeting place with the prized possession by

194

now. He was growing nervous, but suffocated that feeling with several vodka mudslides and a few chicken Caesar wraps - two specialties at his coveted franchise. With Dasher or not, he had already gained enough leverage to get President Knudson's buy-in. Knudson was desperate to gain back control of his country by whatever means necessary. Four mercenaries would have certainly mortally wounded Dasher at the minimum, and thus taken him out of the equation entirely. Not to mention, he had also activated the kill switch on a specific subset of clones and sent them as a precautionary reinforcement for the mercenaries. Dasher was either captured or dead, Popov was certain of that much. The vodka and wraps only functioned to make him that much more confident.

The President continued to perpetuate unsuccessful conspiracy theories via Twitter and the country was plunging even deeper into its already divided habits. Popov sat back and read the most recent string, chuckling to himself. He had this country right where he wanted it. The restaurant itself was fairly empty, save the heavy security Popov hired to patrol the premises and wear the traditional Tilted Kilt waitress garb, which he had grown quite fond of. The guards were all ex-Russian Military; some of the best soldiers in the world were here to usher in a new age for Russia and Communism. Once the United States fell to Communism, it stood without reason that the rest of the world would soon follow. Popov looked at the surveillance camera live streams in the parking lot waiting for the President to get there and conclude the deal they struck days earlier. His vision was slightly blurred, as he had been drinking since earlier that morning. He noted the feeling and promptly ordered a Red Bull vodka to perk himself back up. Though negotiating with the President required only a vague coherence, he wanted to make sure he was sober enough to remember something this legendary.

He scrolled through the feed carelessly, taking several more sips from his cup and making a crude remark to the waitress passing by. She was used to this type of behavior from the brand of people that regularly graced Tilted Kilts across the country: a self-perceived alpha male, the kind of customer who would leave a ten percent tip and sexually harass the waitstaff after a couple dozen Michelob Ultras, the type of guy who woke up on third and thought he hit a triple. He noticed something on one screen and rewound the video - a Dodge Charger sat in the parking lot of the restaurant. The presence of the Charger would not be that alarming for the same reason the vulgar comments did not bother the waitress; that type of automobile was to be expected at a restaurant like this. The timing was suspicious however. It was three in the morning and unless it was just some lonely loser looking to sleep one off or get a little frisky, this meant trouble.

"Alexe, Andrei, go into the parking lot and give a look at that Dodge Charger. I want to make sure nothing is going on," said Popov slurring heavily.

The two men strapped on their AK47s and dutifully marched into the neglected parking lot of the restaurant. Popov looked on eagerly through the surveillance cameras, hoping the Dodge Charger was simply the benign transport for someone with an incredibly small penis. The men circled the car several times, looking above and below the vehicle.

"Sir, nothing out here," said Alexe, in the traditional henchman fashion of not noticing the smashed window of the Charger.

Right when he muttered those words, Popov noticed a shadow, but before he could say anything, he heard an agonizing wail through his Bluetooth headset. Both men had been decapitated and blood flowed through their headless bodies in the same whimsical nature as the fountain at the Bellagio hotel in Las Vegas. Dasher stood with an enormous machete behind the two men, apathetic about the blood saturating his face. Popov noticed an overturned box with the word 'fragile' on it and a set of eyeholes crudely carved into the side and kicked himself for not finding it suspicious before. Absolutely nothing in this restaurant would qualify as remotely fragile. He wasn't nervous yet though; Dasher would still have to get through several more armed guards before even coming close to getting to him. The President was also on his way. If push came to shove, could he convince Dasher to join them? Popov was wasted enough to believe it, but he put the thought out of his mind. He had to trust his soldiers and that they had been trained for this very scenario: Defending a fast-casual restaurant built for perverts from a man who saw himself as the son of God and who would stop at nothing to protect his country.

In the main room, the men took to the windows, blindly firing their AK47s into the parking lot, hoping to get lucky on a stray bullet. On the roof of the facility, Dasher chuckled to himself at the bullets spraying into the neighboring businesses and houses. These soldiers did not stand a chance. Their Russian training wasn't comparable to what he had gone through for the United States military. Dasher entered the facility's air conditioning duct and began crawling. He just had to get to Popov before the President in order to execute the plan he had been preparing for his entire life. The air conditioning duct smelled heavily of lunchmeat soaked in spiced rum. A new, ill-conceived menu item Popov must have been working on. Dasher quietly lowered himself into a back room of the God-awful bar and grill that had somehow captured the heart of the country. He stalked into the main room where the guards had stopped firing and were looking outside aimlessly. This was going to be easy. He sprinted behind the first guard and punched through his back, cracking several ribs and breaching into his internal organs. The man died instantly without so much as a word, but the sickening sound of someone's fist cracking ribs and penetrating organs had raised the alarm of the other guards. They began firing in that direction. Dasher instantly ducked under a table and turned it over, probing for momentary coverage from the fire. He kicked himself for choosing the machete as his only weapon; the several silenced firearms he left back at the hotel would have been handy in this circumstance, but he had prayed on the matter and God had advised him that the machete was the way to go. He had to remain confident in the advice he got from his God. The table, which was bulletproofed according to standard franchising rules of Tilted Kilts across America, absorbed the gunshots easily, but Dasher was in deep. He glanced over at the bar and had an idea that might just be crazy enough to work.

Goat Knuckle Inn,
Washington D.C.,
United States

The rest of the group was just waking up in the motel room at the Goat Knuckle Inn. They had all slept deeply for several hours; the previous days had exhausted them tremendously. The room looked and smelled as it had the night before, which made all of their stomachs turn. The bathroom door was wide open though, and Duke was nowhere to be found.

"Duke?" Kibby asked, pushing the bathroom door open slightly. Duke hadn't flushed the toilet, but otherwise, he definitely was not in the bathroom.

"Wonder if he went out for coffee?" asked Serone.

They all agreed that was probably the case, even though deep down they knew otherwise. Stacy turned on the television so Terry could watch his morning *Veggie Tales*. There was an air of tormenting anxiety in the room that bred with the objectionable smell emanating from the neglected motel room toilet.

"Wish Duke had flushed," said Kibby longingly.

"He never does and he must have made something fierce in there, his bowels only move after murdering, he's been corked up for the better part of this decade," replied Stacy sadly.

Kibby disregarded the comment and returned to the lumpy mattress to sit down and think. He scrolled through his Twitter timeline in an effort to see if anything peculiar was being tweeted about throughout the city. He came across one user, @barstoolguy69forever, who had taped a brief clip of Dasher climbing into a box labeled fragile with an enormous machete outside of a Tilted Kilt restaurant.

Kibby looked at the video several times and expanded the comment thread. People were speculating on whether it was actually Dasher or a deep fake. Kibby knew it was Dasher. He couldn't tell why, but he just knew. He noticed an address in the background of the video and scribbled it down on a piece of soiled legal paper that was next to the bed stand beside a used condom. He called the other two over to watch the video.

"Guys we need to go. What if Dasher needs our help?" asked Kibby. Stacy and Serone looked at each other.

"If he wanted our help, he would have asked for it," muttered Serone, who at this point desperately wanted out of the entire situation.

"He saved all of our lives! We owe him that much. We need to do anything we can to help him!" shrieked Kibby.

Stacy and Serone agreed; though Duke was likely relentlessly slaughtering an entire restaurant of people at this point, and they would probably only serve as obstacles in his end game. Yet, they still felt the unquenchable desire to go.

"Terry, you hang back on this one bud. You've done quite enough today," Serone said in an attempt to stop any suggestion of Terry joining them before it happened, but Stacy agreed. Terry would stay at the Goat Knuckle Inn. They armed him with his customary Desert Eagle 5.0, put on *Veggie Tales*, and left him with a bag of ranch Cheetos. The three ordered an Uber and typed in the address of the restaurant Kibby had noticed in the background of the Twitter video.

17 Duke Dasher Succumbs to Alcoholism

Washington D.C.,
Tilted Kilt Pub & Eatery,
United States

Dasher waited until the firing had stopped and listened for a reload. When he heard the clips drop, he immediately sprung up and did a front flip, seeking cover behind the bar now. Dasher quickly formulated a plan in his head he thought might just be crazy enough to work. The three men reloaded their clips. Knowing that Dasher was desperate, they began slowly walking forward, ready to pin him down at the bar and riddle him with an entire clip worth of bullets for all the trouble he had caused them. Dasher's plan was going against something he had sworn to never do his whole life. Something he was risking eternal damnation for, but if he played it right and did enough penance, maybe he would be forgiven somehow. Sometimes you have to do the wrong things for the right reasons.

He reached over the bar and grabbed a bottle of Bacardi 151, a staple in every cocktail at Tilted Kilt, and took a large pull. The liquid in the bottle bubbled majestically and as he gulped, the bubbles within ascended towards heaven. Salvation can be found in the most unlikely places thought Dasher. He retrieved the book of matches he had gotten from the Goat Knuckle Inn, the only souvenir outside of priceless religious artifacts he indulged in on any trip he took, and arose from behind the bullet-ridden bar. Dasher lit a match and blew the Bacardi as hard as he could and watched as the flame ball engulfed the three men hunting him. He jumped over the bar and kicked the knees of one

203

of the guards the opposite way, shattering his patella before landing an uppercut that destroyed every tooth in his mouth. The teeth sprayed all over the floor; they almost appeared to be liquid given how badly they were obliterated. Using the guard's burning body as a springboard, Dasher leapt to the second guard; where he cut one of his legs clean off with the machete. He then quickly stomped the man's face into oblivion. The sensation of wet sand came to Dasher's mind as he doled out the final blows. He submerged his boot into the muck one last time and shook the facial remains from the treads of his shoe as though he had stepped in dog shit. The third man was still on fire, running around the bar desperately seeking relief for his burning flesh. Dasher whipped the machete at him. It landed directly on the side of the guard's face and put the poor bastard out of his misery - another of Dasher's good deeds. He looked up towards the sky and nodded to the Lord, grateful for his assumed approval.

Dasher walked into the depths of the restaurant where he knew Vladimir Popov sat. As he walked back, he began to feel dizzy. He staggered slightly and his vision was blurring. He leaned up against the bar, not sure what was happening. Had he been shot? He checked his body the best he could and didn't feel any bullet wounds. He then remembered the Bacardi 151 he had used to burn the guards only moments before. How could he have forgotten that loathsome nectar molesting his tongue? Even though he desperately tried not to swallow any of the poison, a few drops must have accidentally been ingested and tarnished his pure body and mind. Was this what being drunk felt like? He wondered and then screamed out in pain. His mind descended into the depths of his subconscious, which housed decades of unaddressed anxieties and fears. He fixated on the singular thought that God would not forgive him for a sin this grave. He looked at the death and destruction inhabiting every inch of the piece of shit restaurant, but then returned his gaze to the bottle of Bacardi...drinking liquor was strictly forbidden under any circumstance. In the middle of his self-reflection, he heard a door creak. Vladimir Popov walked out of his office and began approaching Dasher, who appeared to be in the midst of a full mental breakdown. Popov tripped and stumbled, then rolled into a summersault, mimicking the scene in which Willy Wonka introduces himself to the world from the 1971 version of *Willy Wonka and the Chocolate Factory*.

"Now you know what it feels like Dasher," Popov said as he took another pull from the bottle in his hand. Miraculously, he hadn't spilled a drop during his elaborate entrance.

"You know what it feels like to be drunk and a sinner Dasher, but what does it matter? There is no afterlife you piece of shit coward," yelled Popov, kicking Dasher in the stomach and causing him to collapse onto the ground. Popov laid another flurry of kicks into Dasher, who remained helplessly drunk on the poorly installed shag carpeting of the restaurant.

"You thought you could beat me Dasher! All of your efforts got you here, now look at you!" said Popov, stalking around his body like a lion.

"Your country will be mine Dasher and there is nothing you can do about it. Your President is on his way here to pledge his allegiance to me. Once that happens, I'll flip the kill switch on the clones and we will perform the greatest military coup in the history of the world," Popov continued, spitting a mouthful of vodka on Dasher. He walked behind the bar to pour himself another drink, unconcerned with Dasher in his feeble state.

"Your God doesn't care about you or country Duke. You need to admit that before I kill you and you enter complete and utter blackness," laughed Popov. "Where is your guardian angel now?"

Dasher laid on the ground, wondering if this was it. He didn't believe a word Popov said about the afterlife, but maybe God's plan for him was, in fact, dying on the floor of a fast-casual restaurant at the hands of a drunken lunatic. The clear rum he accidentally consumed muddied Dasher's mind, but he desperately searched for a way out of the situation. Popov had to be stopped by whatever means necessary. He dug deep as the room began to spin. Could one pray themselves sober? It seemed unlikely, but then again, if prayer worked for virtually everything else, could it also work for sobriety? Dasher closed his eyes and began praying harder than he ever had in his life. Popov walked over to the unusual scene and paused to consider the strangeness of the situation. He could not figure out what Dasher was doing, but the stillness of his body almost made him appear dead. Popov could see his chest moving up and down, an indication that he was still breathing, but otherwise, his eyes were closed as though he were deep in sleep.

Popov punched him in the face several times, but the body remained totally still. In his head, Dasher was walking on cotton candy clouds, approaching an enormous, extremely jacked, tanned and bearded old man. Thoroughly oiled up and bronzed, but still unmistakably Caucasian, God was exactly how Dasher had imagined him. Dasher was particularly relieved to discover it was confirmed, a him. Just like he had always believed. He would shove this revelation in Stacy's face the first chance he got. The clouds underneath his feet swirled and elevated him towards the enormous face of the only man Dasher had ever looked up to. Was Dasher to be admitted into heaven here and now? Would he ever return to his earthly form? The beauty was so immense that a part of Dasher hoped this was it for him. He strongly wanted to spend the rest of eternity sliding down the enormous oiled muscles of this omnipotent being. Dasher's hallucinations, caused by only several drops of alcohol, were so vivid that he believed he was about to interact with the all-holy deity he had looked forward to meeting his entire life.

"Duke, you know I could send you to hell for what you've done here," said the giant man sitting in the chair, looking down at the burned and bloody corpses littered throughout the restaurant.

"I know. I shouldn't have taken that drink, but I had to...to save the country from a Communist takeover," Dasher replied frantically, trying to explain the altered state he was in.

"I realize that Duke...and because it was for America, I want you to go back. When you awake, you will be fully sober. I trust you'll know what to do," said the man in the giant golden throne. Dasher nodded. He bowed his head and replied, "One way or another, we'll make believers out of everyone."

Popov had a pistol lined up and pointed it at Dasher's forehead. "I'm done with shenanigans Dasher. The President will be here any minute and you can't be here."

Just as he was about to pull the trigger, Dasher's eyes exploded open. His head instantly shot up and landed squarely on Popov's nose. Popov fell backward; a spray of blood covered the top of the bar. The shock of the blow made him lose a grip on his pistol, which flew into the air. Dasher stood up and cracked his neck once more. Popov rose from the floor, wiping the blood from his nose.

"You didn't think it would be that easy, did you Dasher?" said Popov as he formed a fighting stance.

The two charged at each other and began trading blows - leg kicks, punches, headbutts, attacks, counter-attacks. The tornado of limbs was impressive, as both men tried every technique they could think of to best the other. Popov's drunken nature made him completely unpredictable; Dasher was unaccustomed to fighting someone this intoxicated. For every punch landed, there was another absorbed. They tangled and wrestled throughout the bar, breaking bottles on each other's heads and attempting to strangle each other with varying chotskies they found in the restaurant. Dasher picked up a Stonehenge snow globe and bludgeoned Popov's head with it, but he was too drunk to notice or care. He persisted on, taking a chunk of Dasher's ear with his teeth and spitting it into the air. Dasher sprung up and the two staggered around each other in a circle like wounded animals. Popov approached Dasher for another round of fighting and just as he did, Dasher blew a mouthful of vodka he had been holding in his mouth during the brawl into Popov's eyes. Popov chuckled.

"Do you think that's the first time I've had vodka blown into my eyes you fool?" said Popov, not blinking his eyes once. He grabbed a bottle from the bar and used a bottle of Smirnoff Blueberry like Visine, dripping the vodka directly into his eyes. He blinked them open and grinned at Dasher.

"You didn't think that was just vodka, did you?" said Dasher wiping blood away from his nose.

Popov now blinked several times, his vision blurring more than normal when he was three sheets to the wind.

The blackness was closing in rapidly. He rubbed his eyes furiously.

"What was that liquid Dasher?" asked Popov, beside himself at the shock of losing his vision. His eyes were burning out of his skull. They eventually liquidated and poured onto the floor like a buy-one-get-one vodka mudslide on Tuesdays from 3-5 a.m.

"You actually thought I would let that superweapon you created go completely to waste?" said Dasher.

"After I blasted your friend Addison Beach's head off with a shotgun, I extracted some of that sweet poison you worked so hard to create," Dasher continued to Popov's dismay. "I've been hiding it in a capsule under this tooth, and fortunately for me, my friend Mikel Serone gave me the antidote." Dasher popped the tooth out of his mouth, hurled it across the bar, and took a drink from another bottle with the words antidote written in child-like lettering.

Much like Popov had tried to turn Dasher's God against him, Dasher had now used his perfect weapon against him. Dasher walked up to Popov, who was now swinging around blindly, and lopped off both of his arms effortlessly. Popov was now on his knees; Admitting defeat, he asked for one final sip of vodka. Dasher obliged, slowly walking to the bar and grabbing Popov's preferred vodka, Smirnoff Raspberry, or as Popov adoringly referred to it, Smirnoff Raz. He jammed it into his mouth and Popov slowly drowned in the thing he loved so dearly.
  "I'm not as think as you drunk I am," said Dasher as he let the body fall to the floor. He considered how great the phrase would look on a LiveStrong type rubber band

210

bracelet. He then glanced up at the surveillance screen to see the presidential limo pulling into the parking lot of the Tilted Kilt; he had to make quick work if his plan was going to end successfully.

18 One Glory Hole to Rule Them All

**Washington D.C.,
Tilted Kilt Pub & Eatery,
United States**

An Uber carrying Stacy Dasher, Mikel Serone, Patrick
Kibby and a complete stranger pulled up tentatively
around the corner of the Tilted Kilt restaurant they saw in
the video Kibby found of Duke Dasher. Though Serone
and Kibby objected to riding Uber Pool on the way to
something so dangerous and time-sensitive, Stacy had
insisted that Duke would be furious if they splurged on a
regular Uber. The Uber driver and the stranger peered out
the window of the extremely crowded Toyota Prius. The
restaurant looked like a warzone. There were two
decapitated bodies in the parking lot, the windows were
blown out of the entire restaurant, and there were bullet
casings everywhere.

The Uber driver sheepishly asked if this was their location
and offered them a loose mint from a dirty tray before
reminding them to tip and leave him a five-star review.
The stranger, who had also opted into the unfortunate
pool that day, was sending a selfie of himself with a dog
filter applied that showed the carnage behind him. He
captioned it with "felt cute might delete later LOL!" and
sent it off to his uninterested followers. Serone motioned
for Kibby and Stacy to follow him around the side of the
building. They hugged the wall tight, noticing the
President's limo pulling into the lot.

"Duke must not have been able to get the job done in
time. Even if he's in there wearing Popov's face, there is

213

no way the President and his security detail won't notice the butchery out front," Serone whispered to the others.

However, there was nothing they could do now. They waited anxiously for the brake lights to go off and the President to inevitably discover the plan. The President exited the car with his detail following. Serone was breathing heavily, anticipating the discovery and wondering what the hell happened at this Tilted Kilt hours earlier.

Washington D.C.
United States
(1 hour earlier)

President Knudson's limo ride to his favorite local establishment had been uneventful. He had been happy that Popov chose this bar and grill as the catalyst point for the collapse of America; somehow, it seemed fitting. The most powerful country in the world would be toppled by two men eating buy-one-get-one chicken Caesar wraps and drinking Appletinis in an inexplicably sweaty booth at a fast-casual restaurant with sexually objectified waitresses. He waddled to the limo with more vigor and excitement than he had experienced in the last decade of his life. His right arm grew numb, a daily occurrence for the fearless leader, so he took his left hand and furiously pounded the shoulder until feeling returned. He made a note to check with the White House doctor about the constant sensation, but almost immediately forgot about it. He knew he was healthy. Would an unhealthy man really be able to run a country as seamlessly as he had? The bedsores forming all

214

over his body were a testament to his Presidential conquests. His irregular bowel movements were proof that this country was the best it had ever been. He wondered if Abe Lincoln had made sacrifices as he had for the country he formally loved. Once the agreement was made with Popov, he could rewrite the history books as he saw fit and his Presidential run would last as long as his thinning heart continued to pump blood into his enormous limbs.

He sat in the limo and spread his legs as wide as humanly possible. He learned long ago that spreading your legs out was a sign of class and fortitude. Although, it also helped air out his painfully swollen testicles, which were at the bottom of his laundry list of eccentric medical abnormalities. The prospect of betraying his country would be a lighthearted romp compared to the routine suffering of his everyday existence.

The security guards sat uncomfortably close to the President in the limo, their shins caressing the soaking wet suit pants of President Knudson. The heat in the car was on full blast, which made matters worse for the security detail who were drowning in the scent of stewed cod and burning hair. President Knudson glanced out the window to take in the light snowfall that had started. He loved the way snowflakes glided peacefully towards the earth and the white flakes reminded him of doing cocaine. He imagined himself on Christmas Eve, hovering over a mirror, battling the blood coming out of his nose to muster one final hero loaf of the white stallion before collapsing under an undecorated tree and sleeping until New Years. The limo pulled into the Tilted Kilt parking lot. The majesty of the restaurant immediately consumed him; drool ran visibly out of his mouth. One guard nudged his enormous protruding gut, signifying that it was time to enter the restaurant. President Knudson snorted and horked, seemingly awoken from brief unconsciousness. He stepped slowly out of the car. He took in an enormous breath of the cold night air and exhaled, creating a vast plume. It was a great night to become the most powerful man in the world he thought.

Washington D.C.,
Tilted Kilt Pub & Eatery,
United States

The President and his detail approached the headless corpses and shuffled past them without a second thought. One of the security guards nudged a body with his foot, moving it slightly out of the way to create a clear path for the President, but otherwise, they disregarded the Campbell's chunky soup can full of assorted human remains that stained the snow beneath their feet. The other guard pulled the pilled suit sleeve of President Knudson. The president shopped almost exclusively at Jos A. Bank, and thus his suits were in an eternal state of disintegration. He claimed that the cheap-looking suits made him appear more approachable, but in reality, Jos A. Bank was the only company willing to fit someone who had a fifty-inch waist and twenty-six inseam. The proportions were downright perplexing. Many speculated that his kneecaps had simply collapsed under the weight of his enormous gut, leaving him with unnatural appearing limbs.

The President turned to the guard who just had the nerve to tug on the regal polyester blend of his double-breasted coat on such an important day. Knudson recoiled his elbow away from the guard. He noted to himself to have the man and his family murdered once the new government was in place. Absolutely no one touched his suits, save the odd suit handler, who he locked in the confines of his bedroom. The reality of the suit handler was a fiercely debated topic amongst White House staffers.

Few people had seen the alleged creature who was presumably responsible for steaming and pressing Presidential garments. His existence or possible existence was based solely on the wait staff delivering a nightly meal through a rusted food slot in the President's bedroom and the sound of a rattling cage and pained wailing they heard throughout the dark halls of the White House on a nightly basis. Many of the house staff wondered why there was a need for a quarantined human with the sole task of caring for cheap suits, but they were too terrified about the true nature of the relationship to ask or pursue the matter any further than shoving food through a slop hole.

The guard pointed at the two bodies lying on the ground; they were headless and covered in flies despite the cold temperature. The President looked down at the beige masses and snorted. He dislodged another heaving wad of phlegm from his congested chest and spit it near the bodies; the green membrane was made even more visible by the snow.

The two bodies were of no concern to him.

Vladimir Popov was known to have an extremely short temper, especially after a few blended cocktails or Bartles and Jaymes. For his amusement, he would offer varying restaurant coupons to destitute employees who were willing to play Russian roulette. These two had obviously lost the game and the opportunity to take 20% off buckets of Michelob Ultra with the purchase of the Celtic Bacon Bleu Burger. His mind was also totally consumed with visions of infallible control; this obsession blinded him to the peculiarities about the ghastly parking lot scene. It was the type of power and dominance that most men only dreamed about. His entire sexless life full of varying shortcomings and ineptitudes would finally be rewarded the way it should be. He looked forward to a time when he could sentence someone to death for looking at him wrong. His right arm grew numb with the anticipation; he slapped it a few times with his left arm in an attempt to regain feeling.

He cursed at his lousy heart, blaming bad genes instead of chain-smoking cigarettes, cocaine, and an inhuman amount of organ meat. He needed a drink badly. His genes may have been bad, but a lifetime of casual physical and emotional abuse had not served his insides well. Just as the President was about to perform the biggest coup in the history of humankind, his insides were waging a similar coup inside his wilting frame.

His enormous body lurched forward slowly. If you were a bystander, it would be impossible to determine whether or not he was moving at all, save the scratching sound made by his enormous orthopedic shoes as they dragged

218

painfully through the snow. His guards grabbed him by the forearm and helped him over the small step to the restaurant. President Knudson noted that all of the windows in the building had been blown out; maybe Popov had taken his suggestion to install a stained glass window piece featuring varying scantily dressed and extremely busty Celtic women. If there was a guaranteed way to add class and elegance to a restaurant, it was busty stained glass women.

Serone exhaled heavily. "Did they really not notice those disfigured bodies?" asked Serone, attempting to interpret what he had just witnessed.

"There are bodies everywhere, I suppose," Stacy replied emptily. The brevity and coldness of the statement had a certain weight to it. Each person was momentarily spiraling within their own heads about how insufferable humanity as a whole had become, about the carelessness with which we all operated and the constant quest for an unreciprocated orgasm at any cost. They all shrugged at the same time and shared an enormous feverish laugh at how helpless they all felt. They followed at a distance behind, hoping to catch a glance at whatever was going to happen in the confines of that run-down, vaguely Celtic-themed bar and grill.

After some time, the President finally made it to the door of the restaurant. He touched the rusted knob of the mossy door; the familiarity of its slipperiness warmed his heart. He pushed the door open after some struggle. The country would be his soon enough.

Knudson and his two guards entered the main room with some uncertainty. There were bodies everywhere, significantly more than just a couple games of harmless Russian roulette would generate. Most of them were missing limbs and horribly burned as well. He made a mental note to ask Popov if this was the type of party he could expect once the country was a Communist dictatorship. Not that he needed any more convincing, but he kicked himself for not showing up earlier, as the twisted mass of loose limbs and flesh melting into the shag carpeting seemed like the perfect way to commemorate the day democracy died. He kicked a few of the bodies as a belated celebration. Having not taken part in the actual party, he felt he deserved some type of retribution, and booting a disfigured carcass did just fine.

His eyes turned towards the bathroom stalls and he immediately grew light-headed considering the prospect of the coveted glory hole he had hand-carved himself. He had spent countless lonely hours waiting for an anonymous sexual encounter that never happened, left only to be hypnotized by the craftsmanship on his perfectly whittled hole. A bespoke hole constructed almost exclusively for him. Maybe tonight was the night he thought. It would, after all, make sense given the amount of power he was about to inherit. His fantasy neglected the fundamental principle of a glory hole, which was based not on status or authority, but rather two strangers at the brink of a sexual collapse plunging into the unknown together.

He looked at one body in particular; it had been blatantly placed in the room. The muscles of the face were exposed entirely; the eyeballs appeared to be saucers of milk in the middle of the stringy red flesh, which stuck to the floor like old wiring. The President's mind wandered to the spaghetti, which he had smothered in ranch dressing, and eaten earlier that day. The man must have suffered immense pain before dying. The spaghetti with ranch, on the other hand, was a delectable breakfast. President Knudson heard something stirring in the corner and looked up. A man walked towards him and his two guards. The guards both drew their pistols as the figure approached.

"President Knudson!" said the voice in a friendly, boisterous manner. There was something off about the sound of the man.

"Popov, is that you?" asked the president shakily, checking his boxers to make sure he had not already ruined them. The physical check yielded what he already knew - he had.

"Of course it is Alphonso. Are you ready for this," said the apparition, drawing nearer still.

The Russian accent seemed contrived at best, though then again, outside of his favorite comedian Yakov Smirnoff, the President wasn't familiar with Russians speaking English. Moving with unnatural speed and agility, Popov appeared almost immediately in front of them. His frame was massive; his skin was sickeningly red and bruised, most likely a product of the debaucherous party. A bone protruded clearly from his forearm, breaching the surface like a newborn lamb from its mother's womb. The skin on his face looked tighter than a drum; its stretched nature appeared incredibly painful and ill-fitting. Each movement made pockets of other skin bulge through the rips and tears that consumed his face. It looked as though any of the worn holes were capable of tearing the weakening structure with one wrong muscle twitch. His eyes, oddly enough, sat sunken back, receding deeply into the skin, almost barely visible at all. Two black, shining balls floating in a relaxing, rejuvenating skin Jacuzzi. A white liquid dribbled down his neck at a snail's pace. He reeked like vodka; his breath held the same stale stench as a men's steam room - it was a menacing presence that served to drown the uncontrollable excitement experienced by Knudson moments earlier.

"You look like hell Popov and that means a lot coming from me. I'm not exactly a spring chicken!" President Knudson said nervously. He limply extended his wet hand; his fingers hung towards the floor as though they were cooked noodles. One of the guards stared deeply at the faceless carcass lying in the middle of the entire interaction. Its melted eyes and screaming mouth fixated on the ceiling fan spinning slowly above their heads. He looked back up at Popov and back down at the destroyed pile of flesh.

"Yes, that was vaping accident, electric blue raspberry," said the man with a friendly laugh in his thick Russian accent... "Come and sit President,"

They sat down at a booth and the man ordered one of the waitresses to bring them over a couple pints of Vodka.

The waitress looked like a shell of a human. She was openly weeping, but dutifully brought the vodkas to the table and even used a fake Celtic accent to make them feel as though they were in a traditional Irish pub.

"Nice touch. You run a hell of an establishment Popov. I'll give you that, but do you have a blueprint on how to run a country?" commented President Knudson, leering at the woman's ass as she walked away. "As much as I love this restaurant, frankly, staring at you is making me sick Popov. I am ready to get the deal done. Let's flip the kill switch on those clones and run this country together...the way it should be done!" continued the President.

The engorged burlap sack of stew beef known as the President of the United States had just offered his complicity in the plan to plunge the United States into the red rivers of communism by way of clone enslavement.

"You'll be an advisor, of course, Popov, but I want absolute power. I want to be the face of the new regime," continued the President, again thumping the right side of his body, attempting to stave off what could be the big one. "The money, the women, the control of the clone army...all mine."

Knudson looked closely at the man in front of him. If he was not mistaken, he could almost see teardrops forming within the gaping sunken orifices from which his onyx eyes swam.

19 The Kill Switch

Kibby stared at the footage he had just recorded on his
iPhone. The President just admitted to the biggest scandal
in the history of the world. He wondered what Dasher's
overall plan had been, given that he had no way of
recording the confession. Dasher was always one step
ahead, but now, looking at him sitting in a booth at a
budget-friendly, imaginary luxury restaurant with a face
crudely stretched and glued over his own, he wondered if
Dasher had lost his mind. The legend of Operation Diesel
Fist had been just that, a myth. Seeing him pull the same
stunt in person was both incredibly sad and disgusting.
Kibby wondered how anyone had ever fallen for the tactic
in the first place. Dasher didn't seem to have even a
remote idea of how human anatomy worked. There was a
visible white paste forming just below the chin. Had
Dasher really thought that Elmer's glue could be used as
an effective adhesive for human skin? Maybe everyone was
just that aloof, too concerned with their own personal
agenda to notice a lunatic in a carved-off face
impersonating a Russian spy.

Maybe we were all just too obsessed with forward
momentum to detect a man sitting across from us using a
bad Russian accent and wearing a freshly harvested bloody
face. Kibby reflected briefly on his own shortcomings. If
Kibby hadn't been aware of the plan from the start, would
he have even noticed a mutilated freak sitting across from
him in a booth? How many hours had been lost waging a

war of attrition with an unceasing onslaught of mundane tasks, deriving no pleasure from completing them but instead experiencing a meager, passing comfort before being clubbed back into anxiety and despair by the next pointless chore? Was the momentary relief spent shitting out a regrettable room temperature shrimp cocktail the night before worth the lengthy stomach ache leading up to the frantic discharge? Maybe those small gasps of air taken while circling the toilet bowl as you spiraled into oblivion were filled with just enough purpose to keep you barely satisfied another day in your miserable existence. Though the motion of circling was at least something. The cyclical nature of the tedious daily grind was both killing him and keeping him alive. The blinking cursor on his work laptop was his heartbeat. This recording gave him purpose; it made him feel like something in his life, in the world, could actually change.

Kibby vowed to change things in his life, to eliminate the parts that caused him so much unhappiness, though part of him knew the fleeting promise had no substance to it and was only made with hopes of momentarily euthanizing his wandering mind. He intrinsically knew that he would remain the same, growing distant from friends and family in favor of lazy consumption of content and aimless toiling. Routine and repetition were the most natural forms of escape, no matter how miserable. In another six months, he would be just as oblivious as the President. Sitting across from someone who was clearly wearing the face of another man in a pee-soaked booth at a restaurant built for contemptible failures of humans trying to convince themselves they were eating a fancy meal and stiffing the waitress on the tip.

"Guys...we got him," whispered Kibby turning towards Mikel Serone and Stacy Dasher.

Inside the restaurant, President Knudson circled his tongue on his chapped lips several times, licking off the dead skin and swallowing it aggressively. He looked at the kill switch on the table. It would turn all of the hastily built celebrity clones into a bloodthirsty army willing to do the bidding of whoever controlled the switch. The President had no plans of actually working with Popov and the current opportunity presented itself perfectly. Popov was utterly alone. The excess from the night before had rendered any guard a mangled mess on the cigarette burned carpeting. He just had to wait for the exact right time to have his guards execute this Russian fraud. He would then control the kill switch and thus, the world.

"I've sworn my allegiance to you Popov. What else needs to be done?" asked Knudson, his eyes darting around the room.

He passed an otherworldly fart through his poorly made suit. It instantly sought and filled the nostrils of every man in the room. The thinness of the suit left nothing up to mystery in terms of the President's diet earlier that day, which had included almost exclusively shellfish and several cans of Monster Energy. The man proudly raised his glass and toasted.

"To the downfall of democracy, the rise of communism, and death of snowflakes," said Popov, an enormous grin spreading underneath the now sagging skin around his mouth.

Just as he finished the toast, he whipped the pint of vodka into the face of one of the guards and rolled onto the ground. The guard's nose spewed blood all over the table and his body collapsed next to the President. The other guard stood up and drew his weapon, pointing it at the man who was now standing in the middle of the dining room.

"You son of a bitch!" screamed Knudson. "What the hell do you think you're doing?"

The man's head tilted slightly, like a confused puppy, then straightened. "President Knudson, do you take me for a fool? Your guard had his gun pointed at me the entire time. He was going to blow my balls off the second I handed over the kill switch," said the man, the Russian accent seeming to deteriorate.
"Well, now he's gonna blow that god-awful face off, Popov, because I'm sick of looking at it. Enter the launch code into the kill switch and hand it over, or this man is going to turn your brains into borscht you commie scumbag," said President Knudson over heavy breaths.

"Hold it right there President Knudson," came a squeaky voice from the front of the restaurant. It was Patrick Kibby, followed closely by Stacy Dasher and Mikel Serone.

"We recorded the entire thing: the deal, the clones, you bending your knee to Russia, we've got it all," continued Kibby, holding up his phone in gleeful delight.

President Knudson looked up in a daze. This sniffling little pipsqueak was not going to ruin everything he had worked so hard for. Being tricked by a Russian spy and then convinced to topple his own government with the help of a clone army was by far his most significant political achievement so far.

"Kill them," Knudson calmly said to the guard who quickly aimed his gun at Serone, Stacy and Kibby.

Kibby's urine-soaked pants grew even darker yet; He shrieked in terror while the other two stared on stoically. Just as the guard was about to pull the trigger, everyone in the room heard a detestable ripping noise from where Popov was standing. The President looked up just in time to see the man who claimed to be Popov whip the blood and glue soaked face at the guard. It flew through the air, spewing shards of skin and varying tendons, nerves and Elmer's glue, flapping through the air with all of the majesty of a Frisbee golf disc thrown by a heroin fiend from high school.

The face landed on the guard with a dull thud and he wretched behind its suffocating grasp on his face. The vomit spewed through the varying holes of the face, seeking any crevice to explode from. The guard clawed furiously, attempting to get the face off, but panic had fully set in and he was unable to free himself from the

229

disgusting flesh saucer. He raised his gun under his chin and pulled the trigger; it was the only way to escape the horror.

"Just like the good ole days," said the man who had ripped his face off. "He's gonna have trouble getting into heaven like that. Suicide is strictly forbidden."

The President was now doubled over on his hands and knees, fumbling for a bottle of pills. He desperately needed his heart medication after witnessing the death of the only man capable of saving him from his current predicament. His chest felt like it was caving in. His right arm was completely numb, and he knew if he did not administer his medication soon, he would die at the hands of his own heart. As he grasped the bottle and frantically chewed a handful of pills, he realized that he had heard the voice once before. Duke Dasher. That grisly voice, which oozed a beautiful combination of masculinity and Christianity, was unmistakable. His face was heavily obstructed by undried glue and leftover fragments from Popov's face, but his eyes were brimming with the type of supernatural, self-perceived piety that could only exist inside of one man.

But how, he wondered? How could Dasher have escaped Popov's mercenaries and clones? The probability seemed impossible at best.

"What...awesome...power…" said Knudson, his mouth agape and eyes bursting from his face. Drool flowed freely from his mouth onto the carpet. A monstrous vein in his forehead twitched furiously, itching to escape the diseased skin it had been trapped under all of those years.

"Didn't anyone ever tell you that overthrowing your own government is a sin?" asked Dasher. His large grin was a clear indication that he was unaffected, at best, by the suicide he had caused only moments earlier.

Dasher's statement was immediately followed by the sound of Serone's insides ricocheting off the floor. The substantial amount of liquid splashing on the floor made a loud enough splat for Dasher to look up and finally recognize their presence. Kibby's voice had done nothing to take Dasher's attention from the President before, but the sound of a weakling losing their stomach always suggested an opportunity to ridicule someone for Dasher.

"Serone! Don't tell me you had one too many Fireball Whiskey-infused Pringles from the hotel minibar last night?" yelled Dasher jokingly.

He walked towards the President and took the gun out of the dead guard's hand. Serone, Stacy and Kibby approached the chaos ahead. The amount of killing Dasher had done in such a short amount of time was an incomparable monument resurrected for the worship of violence and bloodlust. The President sat sadly on the floor like a scolded child. His enormous legs crossed over each other. He hoped for a quick death, but judging by the state of the other abused corpses strewn about, he knew it was wishful thinking.

"We did it, Dasher. We got it all. Once I turn this video recording over to the people at TMZ, it'll be slotted in immediately after their celebrity nip slips segment and we'll have exposed the biggest conspiracy in American history," Kibby said showing the phone to Dasher.

"Say, what was your plan if we weren't here to record it anyway?" Kibby asked curiously. Dasher's face still had flecks of skin, blood, and Elmer's hanging off it. He flicked one of the pieces of loose skin and it landed fortuitously on Kibby's phone; he instantly shook it onto the floor.

"I never think that far in advance Kibby," laughed Dasher, as though the question were somehow unreasonable.

"Dasher, listen to me...in your hand, you hold something that could give you more power than anyone in the history of mankind. Genghis Khan would look like Ross Perot. If you hit that switch, you control an almost unlimited amount of clones who will do your bidding. I could guide you Dasher. I could help you," groveled President Knudson, reaching and holding onto Dasher's ankles.

"Imagine you and me, forcefully instilling your Christian ideals on this country. Imagine raising young Terry in such a beautiful country!" continued Knudson. Dasher brought the pistol up and whipped Knudson hard in the face. Knudson spit up a heaving mouthful of indistinguishable bone fragments.

"Keep my son's name out of your mouth, you sick piece of crap," replied Dasher.

"But think about the possibilities Duke: secure borders, one nation truly under God. These changing times would halt instantly. You could force the world to adhere to your principles…preserving your way of life forever Duke," the President continued, now ugly crying.

Kibby and Serone looked at each other in disbelief. Could the President really be trying to barter with a man whose moral compass was allegedly dictated directly by God himself? A man who had just been through hell and back in an effort to save the country from the evils of communism? The President looked on hopefully as Dasher picked up the kill switch, which had fallen to the ground.

"You realize your plan would have worked if you would have just let me be," said Dasher calmly. "All I ever wanted was to live a simple life where I could judge people with the same authority as our Lord, and then get fast-tracked into heaven for services rendered for the greatest damn country on earth," continued Dasher.

"A loving husband, a good father, and more patriotism in my big right toe than you have in your entire pathetically obese body," continued Dasher over the uncontrollable sobbing beneath his feet.

"Duke, we have what we need right here. Let's leak this to the press and have him thrown in jail forever," Kibby said encouragingly. Stacy and Serone nodded.

Dasher's preaching was getting tiresome to everyone who just wanted out of the nightmare-inducing restaurant. Dasher stared silently at the President, who was still grabbing his ankles. His face was planted on the floor and tears streamed onto the carpet mixing with all of the blood. He wondered how this groveling insect was ever elected to represent the United States. As a Republican, nonetheless, Dasher would have understood if this was a Democrat on the ground, but not one of his own. The snow was drifting gently through the blown-out windows. The restaurant and the warm glow of the streetlights made the dining room almost picturesque, if not for all of the dead bodies and horrible Celtic-themed decor. Everyone in the room listened closely to Dasher's ragged breathing; the betrayal of the President had clearly cut deep for the man who was the self-proclaimed 'greatest patriot to ever exist'. Dasher lifted his leg slowly into the air.

"Duke, just put your leg down. Think about what this means if you do what I think you're going to do. We lose all credibility! This could plunge the country into complete anarchy - the only thing worse than communism Duke! Just think about it," yelled Serone over the howling wind blowing through the restaurant windows.

Dasher looked up at him and muttered, "Wrong choice of words. The only thing plunging is my boot into this man's head." His leg swung down and his heel drove into the

President's head, which caved with the same enthusiasm as a rotting jack o'lantern. Brain matter exploded through the top of his skull like a similarly festive New Year's Eve party favor. A lengthy gurgling sound filled the room. They all waited eagerly for it to stop. Overcome with emotion, Stacy Dasher ran to Duke and threw her arms around him. Kibby and Serone both stood with their hands over their heads, perplexed at how quickly the situation had escalated.

"Duke! Do you realize what you've just done?" shrieked Kibby. Serone remained silent, numb to what was happening around him. Of all the atrocities in the last three days, this was the most heartbreaking. Though he didn't much care for the President, something about the way his melon brains sprayed all over his shoes made this death particularly poignant.

"I just saved the country Kibby...and your soul," said Dasher, walking towards Kibby with the gun pointed at his chest. The next thing Serone saw was the flash of the weapon. Kibby fell to the floor and a red stain began forming on his white Untuckit shirt.

"The United States deserves better," continued Dasher. He approached Kibby, who looked sadly at his ruined luxury business casual fashion statement. The shirt, which had functioned as a personality for him for so many years, was now covered in his own blood. He felt fortunate enough to die in something so fashionably sensible and elegant.

Very few men could say they had been killed in a shirt that looked so good untucked. He desperately hoped the brand would create a shirt in his honor. He would finally be immortalized in something that humanity needed and used every day. He looked around; deep down, he knew he would be forgotten with the rest of the characterless dead goons strewn about the floor. Though he was dying at the hands of a delusional religious fanatic, at least there was some pageantry. Before today, he always assumed he would die choking on reheated Tuna Helper, sending out a high importance email on a Wednesday in February. His social media followers would be proud knowing he died at the hands of one of the greatest heroes in American history. He imagined the posthumous likes flowing in and hoped that whoever had the honor of boomeranging the last drops of blood flowing from his body would tag the Untuckit official account.

Dasher bent down and picked up the phone, which contained all of the evidence against the President, Popov, and the cloning facilities. He held it in his hands, gazing into the blue light for several seconds. His face appeared possessed in its magnificent glow. Dasher assured himself that Kibby's blind faith in this device had ultimately led to his death and he was in no way personally responsible. Serone began slowly walking back towards the door. He wouldn't meet the same fate as Kibby, and though Dasher had called him a friend while they were in the woods, friendships can be confusing when two people are tethered together and hunted by ruthless mercenaries.

He wondered if Dasher had ever really considered him a friend. Was someone who claimed God was his best friend capable of maintaining a remotely functional friendship with another human?

20 The Baptism of Mikel Serone

Washington D.C.,
Tilted Kilt Pub & Eatery,
United States

"Duke, honey, let's all just go home. I bet Terry is worried sick about us," said Stacy, finally managing enough courage to say something to a man who was clearly losing his mind.

"Stacy... Knudson was right, and you know it," said Dasher. "We're not cut out for this world; we're too pure and too virtuous. But it can be reshaped! Reformed to fit us. Burned down completely and built from the ground up with our bare hands! A man-made rapture to cleanse the earth!" screamed Dasher.

"Stop right there, Serone!" he continued, noticing Serone's attempted exit. "I'm going to need a right-hand man, pal...if you were to consider that baptism we were talking about...I could see you making a heck of a Vice President," said Dasher, jocularly pointing a gun directly at him. His tone switched immediately. "You could be purged of original sin in the divine waters of a men's room urinal! Confess your sins to a stranger through an extremely worn glory hole!"

Serone wondered if Dasher was indeed this mad. The years of blind faith, rabid intolerance, and unchecked bloodlust had finally spoiled his brain. Maybe he was a hero at some point in his life, then again, maybe not.

Somehow, being offered salvation by way of a men's room urinal didn't even crack the top hundred insane things that had happened the last several days.

"What do you say Serone? You and me! Taking over the country and using this clone army to impose our will on the population. One more time, for old time's sake, pal," said Dasher, using the same eerily joking tone. Serone considered objecting to the prospect that this scenario had somehow been a previously enjoyable endeavor the two had engaged in, but instead, he agreed to the bathroom baptism, knowing his other option was being shot in the stomach and left to bleed out.

"Splendid! You are not going to regret this Serone! I find that forced converts actually end up loving the faith even more than people born into it!" said Dasher.

 "Stacy, go pick up Terry. He should be here for this," Dasher said tossing her the keys to the Dodge Charger still parked out front.

Serone wondered why a six-year-old would need to see a grown man baptized against his will in the urinal of a poorly run, Celtic-themed restaurant bathroom by someone who definitely was not a priest. Maybe to teach him that most of life, at its best, is just a series of escalating compromises. An endless narrative of shortcomings that pulverize your spine into nothing. Eventually, the will to fight dwindles with each increasingly ordinary interaction and the absence of a spine becomes a cherished luxury. Maybe if you're fortunate enough, the rest of your tired bones melt away too, liquefied after years of enduring the keep warm setting in a shared office crockpot. Later lapped up, digested and expelled by some drooling manager barely capable of wiping their own ass. Your existence is an obedient, beige sidewalk puddle, waiting for the next shit-filled treads of an UGG boot to smother your toothless face as another piece of you mercifully evaporates into nothingness. Something as malleable as a puddle in a hole does not feel or desire to feel. It has no desire at all. It does not know comfort and it is neither happy nor unhappy. It pays no mind to the absence of bones or personality. It simply is until it is not.

Serone continued onwards down the rabbit hole of discontent, considering the insanity of Dasher's demand. Of everything that had transpired that afternoon, forcing Terry to witness this charade of a baptism somehow seemed like the most insane. In some ways, Serone had begun to grasp the madness of Duke Dasher, but not his desire to subject his child to this. Maybe it was to prove the prospect that we are in a perpetual state of submission. Maybe it was a display of the humiliation we feel from recurring daily losses that is comparable to being outsmarted by a skid marked, masturbating salesmen in your hometown. Being swindled into buying a rotting ground beef goat from a dilapidated yard sale from a bumbling lunatic. The stupidity of wanting the inedible sculpture in the first place, multiplied by being financially outmaneuvered by a pathetic loser who, for one reason or another, never left. Maybe demonstrating that love and aging have opposite trajectories during our persisting demise. More than likely, however, it was merely a man

241

who thought he was saving someone's soul and his desire to impart that hallucination on the son he could barely tolerate.

Serone shuffled in front of Dasher on his way to redemption. They both heard a loud screeching noise from the Dodge Charger outside. Stacy had clearly gotten out of there as fast as she could. "She's as excited for this as I am Serone!" said Dasher, patting Serone's forehead with the nose of the pistol. Maybe he was projecting, but Serone could sense a certain sadness in Dasher's voice. A realization that after the events today, he would never see his wife and kid again. Enslaving a country with an army of clones was the last straw for a woman who had already endured so much. It was a wonder to Serone that Stacy's abandonment of Dasher required this level of excess. He questioned how people's acceptance of escalating pain and suffering often surpassed their aspiration for happiness.

"Ladies first," said Dasher, opening the bathroom door for Serone. A bathroom attendant stood at attention as they entered, inexplicably unaware of the chaos that had ensued over the last several hours in the restaurant.

"Evening gentlemen. Stall four has a glory hole to die for! Let me know if you need any mints or Stacker 2 diet pills. I'll be right over here if you have any questions," said the attendant, smiling politely.

Dasher grabbed the man's throat and crushed his larynx. Altoids sprayed from his mouth like a winning slot machine. His tiny body folded, knocking over an empty tip jar. "Bathroom attendants are worse than prostitutes in the Lord's eyes. I did him a favor," said Dasher, not even looking at the deflated attendant on the floor.

The bathroom walls were covered in decades of old boogers, which raised off the beige paint job, making it look like the many hemorrhoid ridden, skin tagged asses, which had expelled nutrient-deprived bowel movements into the ill-repaired toilets. Serone's stomach heaved, but there was nothing left to donate to the tiles that were already wealthy with indescribable fluids. He noticed one of the stalls covered in scratch marks, something either trying to get in or out. He saw a poster advertising a Hairbangers Ball residency starting next Saturday and wondered if anyone in attendance would notice or care about the dead bodies.

"This is it huh, Duke? Once I'm baptized and saved, you type the code Popov gave you into the computer kill switch, activate the clone army and rule the country under a fourth grade understanding of the Bible?" asked Serone, who had been swaddled in a white table cloth by Dasher, a traditional baptismal garb generally reserved for actual babies.

Dasher was now dragging Serone across the sopping wet tile of the bathroom on the way to what he claimed to be the urinal where many great men had been baptized before him.

"We, Serone, we. You are my oldest friend and confidant

after all! We'll cancel woke culture. We'll make women illegal. We'll make *My Sacrifice* by Creed the national anthem. Any carnal urges will be punishable by death. We'll demolish the White House and turn it into a golden calf. If people look at it, that is also punishable by death! The snowflakes will melt again Serone. The glory of God will penetrate this country once more and shakily thrust until it climaxes its seed of redemption all over the sinners!" Dasher said, his head cocked and turning towards Serone who lay helplessly on the floor.

"Some of the most important Americans in history have been baptized in this urinal Serone! You'll join a pedigree of fine men and soon you'll be leading a modern-day crusade with me and you'll have guaranteed entry into heaven! George W. Bush was saved by this same purifying waterfall!" continued Dasher, wrestling with Serone's body as he attempted to get it in line with the urinal from which the holy waters would cleanse his scalp.

Serone wasn't familiar with Christianity or traditional baptisms, but his rudimentary knowledge lead him to believe that his head would be facing upwards with the water washing over his forehead. Instead, his head was shoved into the asparagus pit of the urinal, his mouth pressing firmly against the urinal cake, which the attendant seemed to have forgotten to replace for the last decade. He heard the sound of Dasher's hand aggressively pulling the creaking toilet handle multiple times. Scalding hot rust water blasted over the back of his head. Serone yelled out in pain, but Dasher could not hear him. He was singing at the top of his lungs in jubilation, "Our God is an awesome

244

God! He reigns…from heaven above!" Each time the word *reigns* was sung, another blast of water christened Serone's scalp. The sound of Dasher's voice suggested a genuine happiness for what he was doing, a sincere compassion for the only friend he had ever had and his quest to save that friend from eternal damnation. After what seemed like hours, Dasher turned Serone over, apparently appeased with the scientific number of urinal flushes it took for a proper cleansing baptism.

"You did it pal. You are saved. You were so brave," Dasher said to Serone, whose eyes had closed. His face wrinkled even further from the onslaught of water. Dasher was elated at his stillness; oftentimes, the ceremony was so peaceful that the baby or unwilling adult would fall asleep, dreaming of heaven. He laid Serone on the floor once more.

"Hey Serone, wake up, you ole dog, we've got millions of others to save!" said Dasher hopefully. He walked over to the sink and filled a cup full of water, splashing it on Serone's unmoving face.

"Alright Serone, that's enough. I'm starting to get pissed and you will not like me when I'm pissed," continued Dasher. Dasher walked over to the body and booted it; the ribs collapsed instantly. He bent down and hastily tried to pop them back out, fumbling around Serone's denim jacket.

"Not you too Serone," Dasher said calmly. He walked over to the counter again and retrieved a handful of Stacker 2 diet pills. He shoved them into Serone's slackened mouth and grabbed the bottom of his jaw, pushing it up and down in an attempt to chew the pills. The pills remained in his mouth, but some of the soggy bits spilled out onto the tile floor.

"How could you abandon me too Serone?" whispered Dasher.

"I forgive you Serone. Some people just weren't cut out for this life. I'll see you up there buddy," said Dasher as he pointed towards the ceiling.

Dasher considered how lucky Serone was to have been baptized. If he hadn't, and had drowned in a similar fashion, he would be rotting in hell. Dasher walked back out to the main floor. He grabbed the computer kill switch and a bottle of liquor and walked back into the bathroom with a bottle of Bacardi 151. He dumped the entirety of the bottle on the swaddled corpse of Serone. He lit a match and tossed it, setting the body ablaze. Dasher sat on the floor next to the fire with the computer in his hands. The quest that started in an effort to save the country, had morphed into something entirely different, something almost indescribable. It was not a personal journey of self-discovery, as there was absolutely no internal reflection or change. It was undoubtedly not a redemption story, as redemption stories require something worth redeeming. A revenge story perhaps, but even revenge has some realm of limitations. It may have been a holy mission dictated by some omnipotent force that only Dasher could interpret. More than likely, it was simply a man of little consequence who had lost everything and now demanded more than his perceived fair share back.

21 Salvation

Washington D.C.,
Tilted Kilt Pub & Eatery,
United States

Dasher opened the computer kill switch and typed in the code Popov had given him. He stared into the screen. Acquiring this computer had cost him everything he loved - everything earthly that is. Dasher thought about his higher vocation. Although God hadn't explicitly told him to use Russian clones to forcefully resurrect Christianity, he was certain it was something He would have wanted. Some things could be assumed. Everyone should go to heaven, whether they like it or not. The green button flashed on and off several times. The light hypnotized Dasher, who wrestled with the decision. If he didn't push the button and gain control of the largest clone army ever constructed, he would have a lot of explaining to do to law enforcement in regards to the body count at Tilted Kilt Bar & Grill. If he did push the button, the world was his, and everyone would worship him like the extension of God he considered himself to be. His thumb hovered around the button before resting on it lightly.

The button slowly pushed in. The feeling of it receding into the device was deeply satisfying. Dasher heard a click and the power shut off in the restaurant. He looked outside and every streetlight was off, along with every light in every house. Moments later, it all powered back on. The blinding fluorescent lights shone down as a sign from God that He approved. Dasher felt like he was floating above the stained carpet; it was the closest to God he had ever been. There was a pound at the door. Dasher looked up, half expecting to see Stacy. Instead, it was the entire cast of the show *The Real Housewives of Gary Indiana*. He grinned as more pounding and more clones began to appear in front of him.

Hundreds of clones gathered and knelt at his feet awaiting instructions. He parted them like the Red Sea and glanced out the window. Tens of thousands more stood at attention outside of the restaurant, more than the eye could see. Helicopters circled overhead, sirens wailed; neighbors of the restaurant looked on terrified from locked windows. Dasher walked into the back of the restaurant and climbed the maintenance ladder to the roof of the building. He stood in front of his clone army and started his proclamation.

"May peace be with you," said Dasher.

"And also with you," the army responded in unison. Dasher knelt on both knees, his hands stretched to the sky. Snow swirled around him and the spotlights from the helicopters focused directly on him. For the first time in his life, he cried. This was happiness. This was purpose.

A preview of Mark Baldacci's next novel, *Harvest*

Daniel Thomas is a man of esteemed ordinariness. He stands around 5 foot 8 inches tall, weighs about 156 pounds, and has size 8.5 feet, though someone had once mentioned they thought his right foot was slightly larger than his left. The light brown Mossimo shoes purchased from Target are somewhat snug. His frame is rather thin, but unfortunately, pear-shaped in a way. The polo shirts he wears with his slightly baggy pleated khakis fit in an unnaturally boxy way. It is likely the cheap material. His hands are wholly unblemished and softer than warmed cotton candy. They have never built or worked on anything, and generally remain planted firmly, motionless on a keyboard for 8 to 9 hours a day. Though he does not currently wear glasses, he has been told his eyesight is deteriorating, and in about four to five years, he will likely go in for a checkup where they will ask him to come back in four to five years for a checkup. His hair is the color of a cardboard box that was once rained upon and has since been dried in the oppressive August sun several times over. It has the same texture too.

His haircut is unmemorable at best, though he has a slight crush on his stylist at Sports Clips, who regularly convinces him into the same cut, and the VIP treatment. For a modest 20 dollars extra, this treatment gets the customer a brief hand massage and a "free" comb. This splurge provides transcendent contentedness for Daniel, though he often only tips two dollars. His teeth are relatively straight. There has been some deterioration of the enamel on his teeth. After significant research, he bought the CVS brand of an enamel strengthener because it was three dollars cheaper than the name brand. "Why would I pay three dollars more for the exact same product?" thinks Daniel, even though the products are nowhere near the same. His favorite band is U2, but he never tells anyone that.

His favorite TV show is *Last Man Standing*. He also enjoys the remake of the television show *Dallas*, arguing with anyone willing that the original didn't capture the essence of Texas. Favorite comedy of all time is *My Big Fat Greek Wedding Two*. Most of his jokes are movie quotes. A bizarre eagerness behind the delivery of said quotes generally makes everyone uncomfortable. Daniel is employed at a company of around 2,500 people, most of which he does not recognize. He sits in a cube, in relative solitude and is generally satisfied producing and deploying emails for products he does not understand. These emails sit in inboxes for several moments before being discarded by the uninterested customers who are routinely bothered by them. Too lazy to unsubscribe, the vicious cycle will continue until either Daniel or the customer dies. In other words, Daniel Thomas is 29 years old, has two first names, and he and his existence are emphatically forgettable.

It's a Tuesday morning in the middle of February around 7:20 a.m. Daniel is tiredly climbing out of the twin bed in his five-hundred square foot studio apartment. Though the apartment is generally tidy, this morning, a pair of pants lie on the floor, and three dirty dishes lay in the sink. This disturbs Daniel to no end, but he is unsure why. A nuisance like this should not cause such tremendous irritation. Casting these feelings aside, he looks in the mirror, noticing an immense paleness that has settled in and momentarily considers the tasks for the day. Picking his nose, rolling and examining the crumb, pondering the perpetual task list in his head. He yawns, emitting a more objectionable morning breath than usual and brushes his teeth. He neglects to brush his white tongue as he usually does. It is undetermined if Daniel is hungry or nauseous. He had gone out on Saturday night with a couple of people he considered friends or at least people that seemed indifferent to his presence. One thing led to another, and the night ended in an agreeable blackout. It was both satisfying and disappointing. Satisfying because he had gotten drunk, frustrating because nothing extraordinary happened. Though nothing really ever happened. "The effects of Saturday's excess must be still lingering," thinks Daniel taking note of the war being waged in his stomach. The decision is made to skip breakfast for the morning, the risk isn't worth it. He had leaked out an eye-stinging gust on the train weeks earlier that had fetched disapproving looks of everyone else in his car. Opting not to shower, he pulls on a pair of black socks, khakis, braided belt, and a striped button-up shirt that causes his neck to itch. It has always done this, but it is generally forgotten until he leaves the apartment. It has been cold for what seems like an eternity. A maniacal, cruel cold. It pierces through Daniel's layers with ease, penetrating through his dry skin directly to his bones. "The goddamn train better be on time this morning," mutters Daniel, discharging a considerable amount of steam. It never is. All he can think about is getting to work, drinking his coffee, and producing highly disposable digital content.

The train is several minutes late, but there is barely anyone on it. In fact, it is curiously empty for this time. Daniel wanders uneasily in and finds a seat in the back, with an aimless suspicion. Coveted solitude. The next part of this morning ritual is staring deeply at his Facebook, watching the cursor blink repeatedly, and trying to think of an amusing movie quote that will garner him several precious likes. He once posted a quote from *Zoolander* that got him 10 likes. "Hansel...so hot right now...Hansel." he thinks and chuckles silently. The pleasure was immense and just now revisited. Watching the notification bar populate is one of the greater joys in life. Noticing that it is the birthday of someone he knew in high school, he quickly navigates to this person's wall and posts, "Happy Birthday, I hope it's a good one!" A flawlessly executed message. One that could neither lend itself to criticism nor be taken as genuine and heartfelt. As the train grows more crowded, Daniel sinks deep into his seat and turns up the volume on his Skull Crusher earphones. He once saw an ad with basketball player Derrick Rose wearing them and thought they looked cool, but they fit irregularly on his ears. They are rather uncomfortable as well, and the sound feels like it's being filtered through a tin can. Derrick Rose wears them, though, so it is of little concern to Daniel. He didn't watch sports but had overheard discussions about Derrick

Rose in both the office place and on the train and decided he seemed like someone who knew a thing or two about headphones. Daniel wished he had extensive headphone knowledge. His iPhone is filled almost exclusively with songs that are currently running in commercials. Listening to the song from the new Samsung Galaxy commercial, Daniel contests that it got screwed at the Grammys. Or maybe it wasn't nominated at all. If it wasn't, it should have been, and it should have won. The song is enjoyed several more times before reaching the platform, Daniel shuffles around several people so that he is the first to exit the train. Lumbering down the stairs, he walks under the elevated tracks and makes his way into the corridor of his office. The outside of the building contains absolutely no distinguishing features. It is twenty-one stories high with a decent window ratio. It appears as though the window cleaning crew hadn't visited in some time. Void of any personality, it is anyone's guess as to what is going on inside. Though no one ever really guesses, the building is generally passed by without notice. Except for those that work there.

Daniel blasts through the rotating door, pushing it with purpose. Coming up to the elevators, he notices his friend Alex standing motionless. There seems to be a heightened amount of malaise buried deep in the pores of his boyish looking face. His legs are turned slightly in, his face is wind burned.

"What's up?" Daniel asks

"Nada, what's good." he promptly responds, the inflection of his voice made this sound like more of a statement than a question. Daniel stands there confused and, after several excruciating seconds, realizes it is a question.

"Oh, nothing, nothing...Are you going to be busy at work today?" A question that has saved lives in those awkward elevator rides.

"Nah, I shouldn't be too bad, it's weird though, I heard they are implementing this new program in a week or so."

"Yeah? What do you mean?"

"Not even really sure, I think they're going to start having us track our time..."

The elevator mercifully opens and both climb in. There are two other people in the elevator, but they appear to be going to different floors. Daniel wonders for a minute what those people are doing on those other floors; do they have a similar existence? They seemed relatively content, but who can really tell. They may have been having the worst day of their life, but this is all buried in the abyss come 9:00 a.m. smothered by deliverables. Greetings. "Out-of-Office" Replies. Microwaved lunches. Anything that is happening outside the confines of the office is cast aside. Cast aside in a sense, but actually just put on simmer, sometimes compounded by the pressure felt. The office should not be mistaken as a therapeutic escape it is a pressure cooker.

"Tracking our time? I wonder why."

"Yeah, again, not certain, anyways going to be a drag."

"Right, I'm not sure what to think yet, just more rules to follow, I suppose."

"I think the program is called Harvest, so be on the lookout for that email."

The elevator reaches the fourteenth floor and the coworkers exit, departing to their respective cubicles. Daniel settles in, turns on his laptop, and waits for the comforting whir of the computer fan. There is a to-do list carefully scribed on the whiteboard in his cube. Several papers also lie strewn about, printed PDFs from a meeting that he attended…or didn't attend, and these were dropped off for his reference, it didn't matter. A tape dispenser lies on its side, a nearly empty box of tissues, several sticky notes with varying passwords written on them, and a jar of gnarled pens from constant licking and chewing are also there. On one wall, there is a poster of the city of Chicago. He walks to the kitchen and places a Fettuccine Chicken Alfredo Lean Cuisine in the freezer next to the other Fettuccine Chicken Alfredo Lean Cuisines. "Other people must like it as much as me," he thinks. He drains a pot of coffee into his 16 oz. Dunder Mifflin coffee mug (which he still finds hysterical, though no one else has ever really commented) and neglects to make another batch. Strolling back to his cube, he gives several silent nods to other people who allegedly work in the building. They respond in kind, neither parties being able to confirm what the other does, or if they even work at the company. Sitting back at his cube, he spins in his chair to take a closer look at the pending items on the whiteboard. "Harvest, eh?" he thinks, going through a general estimate of how long each task during his day would take.

For some reason, he cannot get that word, that program, out of his brain. It seems to be lingering there, not necessarily making him uncomfortable, but certainly present. That feeling experienced when trying to remember if a door was locked upon exiting. There are several emails, which have been flagged in his inbox for a couple of weeks, but no one has really noticed the missing deliverables. He decides to let them be. He takes a long pull from his coffee and starts replying to emails. "Please let me know when this is scheduled to deploy", "Can you please get me those edits back as soon as you can?", "I'm not sure, I haven't heard back from them yet, let me follow up." all of them ending with "Thanks!" Daniel liked the use of exclamation points, they seemed disarming. After he finishes, he begins testing a website. He is not sure what the site is for, or why it exists, but he does know that he has to click on absolutely everything to test for functionality. If a user happened to come across any error, it would be the end of them all. He enjoyed this part of his job, it was mindless enough, and the time passed by quickly. He also found an odd pleasure when he unearthed any type of defect. A sense of importance. Merit beyond his wildest desires.

Daniel often fantasized about being awarded trophies for such heroic feats. They would be proudly placed next to his precious and seemingly endless collection of participation awards. The day passed with little conflict, as most did. In fact, several weeks passed, following the same relative pattern. Sure, some days had slight variations. Donuts were brought in for a birthday, a new coffee machine was in the kitchen, and there were even discussions about a social committee that would plan happy hours to which no one would attend. For the most part, time passed without anyone really noticing or caring. Until the email came. Harvest.

He received the email at home while watching TV. This was one of Daniel's favorite past times, television. The dim glow was as consistent as the shining sun. It bathed the furniture in its warmth. The only thing more enjoyable than his weekly regiment of shows were the happenings on Facebook. Whilst deciding whether or not to comment on a childhood photo someone had posted with the hashtag TBT (Throw Back Thursday), the familiar synthetic whistle noise on his phone sounded. He had assigned this sound as a notification for when an email was received. Though most emails were put off until the morning, something at that moment caused him to open this email. The whistle had seemed more pressing than usual.

From: Capsule Corporation

Subject: Harvest

Hello Associates,

In an effort to help you become the best you can possibly be, to capture any unrealized potential you may have, we are mandating that you begin logging hours on different assignments. This is a program for you! Logging hours will not only help you as an employee but also as an overall human! Logging hours is a best practice, according to the National Institute of Best Practice Determination and should, therefore, be religiously abided by! Numerous studies have shown that increased accountability corresponds directly with elevated happiness and efficiency! We do not require you log time by the minute, however, if it suits you, that type of attention to detail will be accepted with open arms. Please click here to enter the program and begin familiarizing yourself. The program officially begins tomorrow, and we can guarantee that we are as excited as you are!

Thank you in advance!

The Capsule Corporation Management, Development, Human Resources Dynamic Group of Marketing Initiative Best Practices

The email was straightforward, but the excessive use of exclamation points made Daniel nervous. Disarming. "How bad could it be?" thought Daniel out loud, "Plus, if it's best practice and there is empirical data to support

Harvest, it can't be that bad. I do want to be the best employee I can be, and if this is a contributor to that, then, well, I'll be more than happy to participate." The words came out in a voice and tone that Daniel did not really recognize. He had said to them and thought that he meant them, but maybe not. They seemed lifeless and robotic. An uncertainty was looming, though cast aside for the moment so full attention could be donated to a new episode of Burn Notice. After the program had finished, Daniel flicked off the television and went to sleep. It was a strange sleep, one where at points it doesn't feel like you're actually sleeping. He awoke in the morning from this weird trance like state; completely unsure as to if he actually slept at all that night. The feeling of exhaustion, coupled with the luggage under his glassy eyes, contributed to the belief that he had not slept. He climbed out of bed and adhered to his usual routine, preparing for the day.

Daniel pushed the revolving door as usual, but it was more effort today than other days. There was a considerable buildup of both melting snow and salt stuck to the bottom of each of the panels. He nodded to the security guard, who returned a blank stare, utterly vacant. The odd part about security at the building was, they didn't actually provide any protection. Even if they actually did provide security, what would it be for? To Daniel's knowledge, there wasn't anything of extraordinary value in the building, nothing rare or otherwise coveted. He climbed into the elevator and got off on his respective floor. The office was buzzing this morning, but it was hard to tell what about because everyone was whispering. It was initially indistinguishable, a consuming sound, unlike anything he had ever heard, but one word was audible. Harvest. Harvest. Harvest. The hiss of the word poignantly entered his ear over and over. Not speaking to anyone, he walked to the kitchen and filled his mug up to the very top. The coffee seemed cold, but it didn't matter. This morning coffee was a life force. In the mornings that followed those restless nights, the only real option was to become a weak jittery mess. Allow the caffeine to propel the lifeless body and mind throughout the day. The stomachaches and frequent trips to the bathroom were a small price to pay for the fix. He settled back into his cube and examined the whiteboard behind him, which contained his to-do list. Before he could give it much scrutiny, he was interrupted by a sound behind him.

"Daniel?"

"Hi, Erica."

Erica was a coworker that sat in the cube behind and adjacent to him. She was rather tall; Daniel thought somewhere around 6 feet tall, had long red hair with darker red roots, wore glasses, and had a bulbous nose. She dressed rather casually, generally wearing dark jeans and a v-neck t-shirt. She was relatively cute and had decent breasts according to the societal standards of beauty that Daniel's feeble brain adhered. They interacted around four to five times a week, depending on the week. Daniel generally tried to avoid any unnecessary communication because he found her voice to be on the annoying side. She was in Sales and Daniel regularly had to retreat into his headphones to escape the excruciating conversations between her and the person she was cold calling on the other end. He could hear the wheels of her chair; she was scooting over to his cube.

"So?"

"So what?"

"This Harvest thing is pretty crazy, huh?"

"Crazy, in what way?"

"I don't know! Just like that, we have to log all of our time now?"

"You read the email, it seems fine to me."

"But, like, what do we log? For instance, are you going to log us talking right now? I don't know! I'm just sort of sketched out by the whole thing..."

Daniel was caught off guard, as he had not really considered this. Sure, logging work would be easy, but what else had to be logged? How many hours a day were to be allocated to actual work versus say bathroom breaks or correspondence with coworkers? Should he be recording this conversation? It did take a certain amount of time, but only four to five minutes...were items that small worth logging? Daniel's head started to spin for a moment, but he took a short deep breath and seemed to compose himself.

"Look, it will be fine, I'm sure...just do your work and there shouldn't be any problems." On the surface, he appeared calm and collected, but something buried deep had been rattled. This brief discussion had sown a seed of paranoia, of mistrust, of hesitancy. Latent for now, and currently unbeknownst to Daniel, but undoubtedly present. The day progressed and Daniel dutifully entered his time. This wasn't so bad.

Marketing Email # 1: 25 minutes

Website #6 Testing: 1 hour 35 minutes

Meetings: 1 hour 20 minutes

Marketing Email #5: 1 hour 40 minutes

Daniel inspected the gleaming timesheet and was relatively satisfied. He had done those things and it had taken roughly that amount of time. Several tasks successfully completed. A job well done. But something was wrong. It was already almost 5:00 p.m. and it appeared as though he had only worked for five hours that day. His eyes frantically panned over the names and numbers repeatedly. He had arrived at the office promptly at 9:00 p.m. and didn't recall wasting any time during the day, where did those precious minutes go? That goddamn pest Erica was certainly a contributor, but who else was responsible? He had even only taken a half an hour lunch but for some reason, his timesheet looked emaciated. He had indulged in several bathroom breaks during the day, but nothing was wrong with that...or was it? He had also filled up his water bottle a few times, maybe that was it. Regardless, if that is the amount of time he spent on each project, which is what he should submit. Honesty, above all. Anything else and he would be more grief-stricken than he already was. The timesheet was nervously submitted for the day and Daniel quickly and sheepishly exited the office. Where were these feelings coming from? Why such remorse and regret after the submission. How could a program be manipulating his emotions in this way? He couldn't quite tell, but he didn't like it. He would do a better job in the coming days of mastering these minutes, his efficiency. He had no interest in feeling like a lazy asshole ever again.

The train ride home seemed to take longer than usual. Daniel was blasting Aloe Blacc, "I'm the Man." He had heard it in a commercial for Beats by Dre and immediately fell in love, and what better way to rally his downed spirit. If it was inspirational enough to shamelessly promote headphones, it was good enough for him. It was snowing by the time he exited the train. Large flakes enveloped the platform. He stepped off the train and experienced a moment of unbalance; this wasn't the fluffy whirling snow of mid-December. This was the sopping wet filth of late-February. Daniel thought back to the beginning of the month when he had taken that long look at himself in the mirror, that disgusting paleness. He longed for summer, longed for the sun, longed for friends, but more importantly, he longed to fill out his timesheet correctly.

The apartment was warm upon his arrival. The familiar hiss of the radiator had filled the apartment with a dry heat. The tissues he had been blowing his nose with were often bloody. The TV was instantly turned on. Perfect, his favorite episode of *Big Bang Theory*. A coveted rerun. Daniel unknowingly skipped dinner and fell into a deep undisturbed slumber. He awoke to the frantic buzz of his alarm clock the next day, it was the first day of March, and Daniel was ready for change, eager to become the best employee to ever exist.

Entering the office, the next day Daniel's pear-shaped frame had an indescribable swagger, or so he thought, he was doing everything in his ability to appear confident and collected. He had even worn his lucky pleated khakis and his favorite gingham button-up shirt. In his mind, he beamed with pride but was visible to anyone else that he was a nervous wreck. There were noticeable sweat marks streaking his shirt. His pants seemed slightly dirty. He sat down at his cube and took his usual long pull of coffee. He turned to look at his daily to-do list, glistening on the familiar glare of the whiteboard. "Ok, let's do this." said Daniel quietly and cracked his knuckles. He had seen similar knuckle cracking done in several movies before, and though it seemed incredibly cool, after doing this, he experienced immediate remorse. His fingers now ached and he had enough awareness to realize that he looked like a sniveling cuck. No matter it was time to work. He worked with furious enthusiasm that day, limited his restroom breaks, and eliminated any unnecessary conversations with coworkers (which were pretty much all conversations). The clock at the bottom of his work-issued PC read 4:55 p.m. and he decided to check where he was at in Harvest for the day. Five hours and thirty minutes. His stomach immediately hit the floor. How could this be? He looked back on the day, what had gone wrong? He had improved his time tracking abilities by half an hour, but it still seemed hugely insufficient. Who was looking at these timesheets anyways? Maybe everyone, or no one at all. No telling with Capsule Corporation. Was Erica looking at his timesheets? It was entirely possible. He wondered how much time she was logging but became too suspicious to ask. He would just have to do better. The paranoia was manageable at this point, but something was changing in him. For the first time in his life, he considered the weight of time, its progression, its value. This thought was brief, as Daniel realized he had to get home to watch Suits. He had also been neglecting his Facebook responsibilities. He would focus on this tonight and revisit the timesheet dilemma in the morning.

As he entered his apartment and threw his backpack on the floor, he noticed a mess starting to grow. The garbage had not been taken out in several days and was starting to smell. There were dirty plates in the sink, and he had not done laundry in weeks. He just then realized he had also been wearing the same boxers for the last week. The grease and dirt had made them soft. No matter, the weekend was a day away, and he would get his life back in order then. Daniel flopped on the couch and made sure to retroactively like several statuses and pictures that had been posted days before on Facebook. Satisfying. He then flicked on the television and became absorbed in another one of his favorite shows, USA original comedy *Franklin and Bash*. He wasn't as invested. His brain was spiraling into oblivion. The mess in his apartment, his neglect of constant unnecessary Facebook posting. He hadn't talked to any of his one-sided friends this week either, but mainly his utilization at the office. The weekend was coming though, he would fix this all soon.

He quickly masturbated to a Victoria Secret catalog that he had gotten in the mail and went to sleep. He had neglected to eat dinner again. He awoke Friday morning and resolved that this would be the day he completed a perfect 7.5-hour timesheet, with 0.5 hours allotted for lunch, bathroom breaks, and drinking water. He entered the office, took a long pull from his coffee, and looked at the to-do list on his whiteboard. He wasted no time cracking his knuckles. He worked like the demon god of office efficiency this day. He felt he had accomplished a great deal; the day was nearing its end again. He decided it was time to check Harvest. 5 hours and 45 minutes. Daniel's face went white, he had only added another fifteen minutes! Daniel shuddered. He wondered if anyone else was experiencing the same problem but was again too nervous to ask. He walked around and engaged in several meaningless conversations with different coworkers, no one seemed too abnormal. Except Daniel. In only a week's time, people had begun to notice a difference in his demeanor, his appearance. Small things, extra dirt under his fingernails, some soiling on his shirts. His voice was weaker as well; he always seemed to be looking over his shoulder. Everyone knew Daniel was a little strange, but the introduction of these new ticks was making everyone a uncomfortable. Anyways, the weekend was here, and Daniel was thinking of a nice stiff drink to loosen up after one of the most stressful weeks of his life. The strange part was, the stress seemed self-implied, and the mere existence of this program was shoving Daniel into a complete tailspin, an unforgettable funk.

That night Daniel bought a fifth of Malibu Rum (42 proof) and a 6-pack of Red's Apple Ale. He planned to pregame a bit before meeting his two friends out at one of the nameless bars on Clark Street. He ended up drinking ten shots and two Reds Apple Ales and not meeting his friends out. He was severely intoxicated and decided to open up his work laptop, he wanted to become more familiar with Harvest. No good could come from this, but the Malibu and Red's Apple Ale had Daniel feeling no fear and no pain. The rather objectionable combination had given him the courage he needed. It was time to confront his demons, figure out how to get to those 7.5 hours. The numbers on the screen appeared four times over; it was more disorienting than ever. He stared at them with an unnatural intensity. This standoff lasted an undetermined amount of time, but it seemed like hours. All of the sudden, the room began to violently spin. Daniel frantically grabbed the trashcan in his apartment and forcefully discharged everything he had drank and eaten for the day. Several heaves later, he was overcome with exhaustion and fell asleep on the cold wood floor of his apartment. When he awoke, it was 2:00 p.m... on Sunday. Just like the disappearing minutes during the week, the hours in his weekend had entered the same wormhole. His understanding of time and his grip on reality seemed to be slowly slipping away, but Daniel insisted nothing had changed. He would get to that 7.5. No matter the cost.

In the following months, Daniel's routine followed the aforementioned trajectory. During the weeks, he continued to increase his efficiency at work, and the fullness of his time sheet. The logged minutes sometimes grew by 2 minutes a day, sometimes 10 minutes a week. He was slowly but surely making his way towards the amount of time he coveted. 7.5 hours. The time he desired, that he longed for, that he fantasized relentlessly about. The time that was consuming him. The logs were growing more and more peculiar, as well. Daniel still wasn't sure who was even viewing the timesheets, but it was no matter. God himself couldn't dispute what he was submitting. The accuracy, the attention to detail, was a thing of beauty. Daniel immediately orgasmed in his pants. He hadn't experienced anything this glorious in his entire life. His once paranoia had turned into an obsession. A hobby. A sickness. 1 hour 31 minutes and 26 seconds spent on marketing email #452. 1 minute and 23 seconds spent speedily forcing a dump out in the employee restroom. He could cut that time. 23 seconds spent sharpening a pencil. 15 seconds picking a wedgie. "Should this be logged?" considered Daniel momentarily. Of course, it should be, it

274

was at work, and it was contributing to the 7.5. The list went on with a similarly eerie attention to detail. Some of the logged items became too heinous to describe.

The spike in time logged was coming at a cost. Not only were the submissions raising some serious alarms with management, but also Daniel had become a complete recluse at work too. His cube was a disaster. Overrun with Lean Cuisine boxes, Gatorade bottles full of tobacco spit (which he had taken up), what appeared to be thousands of legal pad sheets of paper covered in illegible chicken scratch, and perhaps most disturbingly a litter box, though no animals were allowed in the office. Coworkers had ideas about what occurred in that litter box, but no one really cared to discuss it. The overwhelming smell of piss and human excrement said it all. Later, the litter box disappeared, but the sagging bulge in the back of Daniel's khakis suggested he had found an alternative way of using the bathroom. Physically, Daniel could not have appeared any worse, either. He was no longer pear-shaped; in fact, he really had no shape at all. Gaunt and sunken were the only words people used to describe him. There was a vacancy in his eyes whenever anyone did try to talk to him. He looked somewhat jaundiced. His complexion could not have been fixed with a belt sander. It was a similar texture to the gravel in the parking lot outside. His clothes were tattered and excessively soiled. In fact, one coworker had mentioned not being sure the last time they saw Daniel in a different set of clothes. The pleated khakis and gingham shirt, that was it. He spoke in mumbles and garbles; he had not muttered an audible word in several weeks. Maybe it was the thick white film that had developed on his tongue. Or he was still polite enough to not subject anyone to the horrible odor that resided in his mouth. His apartment followed the same suit. He would return there at the end of the day and flop onto his bed that had long since lost its sheets. He would rest in the filth and stare exclusively at the television, he had gone MIA completely on Facebook, and he didn't care. Absolutely everyone in the office wanted Daniel gone, but no one knew how to make it happen. They were vastly unsupervised, unaware of who if anyone had the authority to actually fire Daniel. There were endless conversations, discussions, and meetings that resulted in nothing as conversations, discussions and meetings oftentimes do. Outlook calendars filled with emptiness. Reaching the perfect 7.5 hours had come and gone, an achievement that he thought would be more celebrated. The uncanny part was no one really noticed. Those time sheets that Daniel had poured himself into lay neglected. Submitted into the abyss. Would they ever be viewed? Was there a real human on the other end of Harvest? Did they care about Daniel? Daniel didn't notice either, he was on to the next. He was now working on logging a perfect 24 hour day. He was as close to an unfeeling machine as a human could get. As he lay in his filth, Daniel couldn't remember the last time he had slept, maybe he was always sleeping. He hadn't really noticed any change in his life, even though everything was deteriorating both inside and outside. His alarm clock sounded and he packed his bag to go to work.

It was November of the next year. November 12, to be exact. But this was irrelevant to Daniel, he was only concerned with the hours and minutes in a day. Daniel sat giddily in his apartment of filth. Atop a throne of empty bean cans and beer bottles. A stupid smirk plastered permanently on his face. His cracked lips desperately clung to his translucent teeth. He would laugh severely and uncontrollably for minutes at a time. A laugh that sounded like it was perpetually breaking up phlegm. Every minute was always logged. The television was on, but Daniel wasn't even certain what he was watching anymore. His eyes mostly remained glued to the ticking seconds in Harvest. He found unrestricted joy in watching these seconds tick. No matter what he was doing, they were always ticking. Always with him. Providing him company. Driving him on. He cherished the timer, spoke with it, and adored it. His alarm went off, which triggered something in his now languid disintegrated brain. It was time for work. He went to work, stared blearily at his whiteboard, took a long pull from his coffee and started logging his hours for the day. Avoiding interactions was easy at this point since no one had any interest in speaking with him. The litter box and diapers took care of bathroom breaks, and he had invested in an IV to eliminate the need for water breaks. Another flawless 8-hour day spent on marketing campaigns that were more important than his existence. Life-changing marketing campaigns. He exited the office, retreated home and turned on the television, tracking all the while. At 11:59 p.m., he peered down at the clock at the bottom right-hand corner of the screen of his work-issued laptop. At 12:00 p.m., Daniel had done it. He had tracked every hour, every minute, every second of the day. He sat, staring at his masterpiece. A work of art that rivaled the most brilliant composer or painter. This was something worthy of worship. An altar resurrected to sacrifice in the name of efficiency. A tear streamed quickly and uninhibited down his dirtied face. His breaths became short and ragged; he couldn't take his eyes off the computer screen. It was almost too much beauty. He knew what fatherhood felt like, as he stared at his perfect creation. He was blissfully in love. Nothing could take his eyes off the computer screen. Just as he was reaching climax, his alarm clock then sounded. He paused briefly, and shut the computer screen, packed his bags and went to work. He sat in his cube, took a long pull from his coffee and examined the whiteboard with his commotion list for the day. He started the timer and began working once again.

Made in the USA
Monee, IL
08 January 2020